BOOK 4 OF THE NYMPH SERIES

Savannah Sacrifice

DANICA WINTERS

author of *Winter Swans* and *Montana Mustangs*

CRIMSON ROMANCE

F+W Media, Inc.

Published by
Crimson Romance
an imprint of F+W Media, Inc.
10151 Carver Road, Suite 200
Blue Ash, OH 45242. U.S.A.
www.crimsonromance.com

ISBN 10: 1-4405-7971-7
ISBN 13: 978-1-4405-7971-4
eISBN 10: 1-4405-7972-5
eISBN 13: 978-1-4405-7972-1

To Carlene and Bingo.
Thank you for all of your love, support, and laughter.

Acknowledgments

There are many people who have worked to make this book and this series possible.

First and most importantly, thank you to my fans. Your love of my books is what keeps me writing. There is no greater feeling than meeting a reader who has enjoyed something that I have had the special role of creating.

Special thanks to the Crimson Romance staff: Julie Sturgeon, Tara Gelsomino, and Jess Verdi, and to my agent, Amanda Luedeke. I appreciate all of your hard work and passionate dedication to the craft of writing.

Acknowledgements couldn't be complete without thanking the man in my life, Herb. Thank you for always listening and helping to be my "idea man."

Chapter One

It was a strange feeling to know that she was probably going to die and to not really care. The last year of Starling Jackson's life had been filled with ghosts, lies, her mother's murder, and the death of an enemy—a death fraught with dangerous threats. Finally, the time had come to make her stand against her world and the ghosts and enemies who inhabited it, even if that stand cost her the only thing she had left to give: her life.

She walked through the Savannah/Hilton Head International Airport and to the baggage claim area where a cluster of people moved in a precarious dance of personalities, the boldest of which pushed to the front of the group while the rest escaped to the far recesses of the room. Starling stood in the middle, pushed back by those struggling for a place at the front and nudged forward to stand as a barrier from the melee by those who hated the entire situation.

Don't let them push you. You are stronger than this ... take control, the familiar voice of the ghost Asclepius echoed in her mind.

"Oh, I'll take control." Reaching into her bag, Starling took out her pills and swallowed down a tablet. That made six. Or was it seven pills today? Regardless, it was a new record. There was no doubt the medicine was losing its effect in keeping the spirits at bay. If she didn't find the *Libros Umbrarum* books soon, there wouldn't be any break from the endless whispers and threats of the ghosts that invaded her reality.

I'll be back ... You will have to listen to me soon enough ... Asclepius quieted.

"Not if I have my way." She dropped the bottle back into her bag.

The stainless steel belt that carried the luggage whirred to life, making the fickle, but telling, dance intensify. Bags poured out into the center of the terminal, forcing some of the meek travelers to come forward and try to grab theirs before the suitcase disappeared into the abyssal baggage carrier's area. Starling's black bag, identified by the red and white ribbons tied to the handle, made an appearance.

She moved forward, readying herself to catch the bag the moment it passed her way. It moved closer. But before she could grasp the handle, a man stepped forward and lifted it off the conveyor. His long, dark hair touched his collar, leaving an oily residue on his white shirt.

"Excuse me!" she called, trying to struggle through the crowd fast enough to see the face of the man who had stolen her luggage.

The man didn't turn. Either he was oblivious to the fact she called out to him, or he was trying to get away before she had the chance to cause a scene that would get the airport security's attention.

"Hey you!" she called, people turned and looked at her like she had lost her mind. Normally their glances would have shut her up, but this time, with so much hanging in the balance, she couldn't afford to let their disapproval staunch her attempt.

The ribbons on her suitcase swayed merrily as if waving goodbye, but their subtle action only made her struggle harder.

"Stop, sir!" she called, but the man only sped up.

Three more strides and he would be out the sliding glass doors. A black SUV was parked at the curb, door open, like it waited for the man. She couldn't let him get away. If he did, she would be left with nothing except her paperwork, a few pills, and barely enough money to get a cab ride and a cheap hotel for a few nights.

She lunged toward her bag, grabbing the ribbons as if they were the bag's lifeline.

The man looked back at her with his storm-colored eyes, and for a split second she could do nothing but stare at him. She tried to memorize the hard arch of his thin lips, his Roman nose, and the widow's peak speckled with gray. He jerked the bag and she tried to hold tight, but the ribbons pulled through her fingers, leaving only paper cuts in their wake.

"Stop!" She lurched forward, ignoring the searing pain in her fingers as she tried to grab one of the bag's handles. The thick polyester fabric scraped against her finger tips, but she missed the handle and her foot struck the end of the bag as it came to an unexpected stop.

There was a strangled noise as the man suddenly fell to the floor. Standing in front of him was Jasper, his slightly too-long chestnut hair in his face and his fist still extended from stopping the thief. The door to the black SUV slammed shut and the car took off with a screech of tires.

"Jasper?" She grabbed her bag but didn't take her eyes off the man who had regularly visited her dreams over the last months. "What're you doing here?"

"Saving your ass. I can't believe you would just leave Vegas without telling anyone. If I weren't here, you would've been screwed." He glanced down at the thief. "You found trouble already. You have no business being here alone."

Airport security rushed through the baggage claim area toward them and stopped beside the man on the floor. "What happened?" a heavyset guard asked.

"The thief tried to steal my bag," Starling said, twisting her suitcase for them to see. "My *friend*," she said, motioning to Jasper, "stopped him." She tried to sound thankful, but after the tongue-lashing Jasper had delivered, she couldn't help stop the anger from seeping into her tone.

"Do you know the man who tried to steal your luggage?" the guard asked as another security officer pulled the thief's hands behind his back and zip tied them.

"No."

The thief lurched forward trying to pull out of the guard's grip. "Get off!"

"Do you have any idea why he would have tried to steal your bag?" the guard asked.

Telling the man the truth—that a group of vulture-shifters was out to get her and her supply of GX 149, and the man at her feet was likely a shape-shifter—seemed like the worst possible answer. She didn't have time for anyone else to think she was crazy.

"I don't know," she said, trying to add a quiver of fear to her voice so the guard would empathize with her rather than question her as to the thief's motives. "He just came up and took my bag. I was so scared," she said for added effect.

"I think I need to get her out of here," Jasper said, wrapping his arm around her. "It looks like this has been quite a bit for her to handle. You won't need her for anything, will you?"

"No, we will handle this man. That is, unless she wishes to press charges." The guard gave her a questioning glance.

"No," she answered. "I just want to get out of here and away from him." She tried to focus on the guard and the thief, but most of her attention was centered on Jasper's hand, warm on her arm. It could have been her fear, or the adrenaline, but she desired his touch. Before the unwelcome feeling grew, she pulled out of Jasper's hold. He didn't need to think she was weak, or worse, that she wanted him to touch her.

The thief struggled. "The bitch is lying! I didn't take her bag! It's mine."

"Really?" the guard asked, with a raise of his brow. "Where were you traveling from?" He looked at the white baggage ticket stuck around the handle.

"Vegas. Let me go."

"Where were you traveling from, ma'am?" the guard asked, turning to Starling.

"Vegas. The guy is lying. I swear I didn't see him on my flight. He knew this was my bag. Or does he tie white and red ribbons to his bag as well?"

The guard motioned to the other guard. "There's only one way to solve this," he said, kneeling down and unzipping the luggage. "What's on top?" he said without opening the bag.

The blood rushed to Starling's face as she thought about the mass of second hand clothes and cheap shoes inside. "There's a gray sweatshirt with a University of Montana logo and a red dress."

The guard looked to the thief. "You want to venture a guess, or just admit that you intended on stealing the woman's bag?"

"I didn't *intend* on anything," the thief retorted.

The guard opened the bag and gave Starling a look of validation. "Are you sure you don't wish to press charges?" He slid the zipper shut.

Starling shook her head. "I just don't want him to do this to someone else."

"Don't worry, ma'am. We'll look into this and make sure this type of thing doesn't happen again."

"Thank you, sir," Starling said.

"Let me escort you to a cab." Jasper leaned in closer. "Hopefully we can get that far without you getting into any more trouble," he whispered.

She turned away from him, and pulling her bag, made her way outside and into the muggy midsummer Savannah heat.

"Did you know that man?" Jasper asked from behind her.

"No. Did you?"

Jasper stepped beside her. "No, but did you see the vulture tattooed on his arm? I have to assume he was one of your shapeshifter friends. Maybe a Catharterian."

She watched as the security guards dragged the man through the crowd of rubber-necking bystanders. "The Catharterians couldn't possibly have known I was here already, could they?"

"They would do anything to learn the reason behind the births that have taken place in the nymph culture. He knew you flew in from Vegas. And I knew you were here … "

"So you are saying you followed me?" After their trip to Vegas, Starling had imagined him coming to her rescue like he had for Harper, her new stepmother, but she hadn't thought it would ever come true. Jasper had disappeared without so much as a phone call or a note that indicated she was anything more to him than a forgotten ward. Since then, she'd spent the last months trying in vain to forget him while she, Harper, and her father, Chance, moved to Vegas for her father's job at the Bellagio's poker tables.

"You didn't think I would let you go traipsing around the United States without protection, did you?"

"It's been six months. I thought you'd gone back to the Sisterhood."

"You know me better than that, Starling. I'm not about to leave you when you could still be in danger."

"Actually, I barely know you at all," she retorted. For a brief moment in time, she had thought otherwise. In Vegas, she'd thought he'd cared for her when she'd seen the spark of attraction, and they'd spent one glorious night in deep conversation. Yet, looking back, he'd never told her anything about who he truly was aside from a bodyguard. "I haven't seen you since we left Vegas. If you've been around, where've you been?"

"I wouldn't have been doing my job if I'd been at your elbow the entire time," Jasper said, a hurt look on his face. "Sometimes the best thing a bodyguard can do is not to be seen."

"Ha. Right. Whatever you need to tell yourself," she said, trying to control the anger that bubbled up with each passing second as she recalled the emotional rollercoaster she'd experienced since he'd left.

But more than anything, she was mad at herself. She shouldn't have allowed herself to feel anything for the man who'd been sent to protect them. He'd only been doing the job he'd been given by the Sisterhood, the governing body for nymphs, by keeping her out of the line of fire in Vegas. If that meant leading her around by her hormones, he must have thought it okay, but she should have known better.

"Look, I have to do whatever I need to keep you safe. The last few months, that meant looking into the vulture shape-shifters, Catharterians, trying to find out more about the extent of Dr. Redbird's involvement in the organization, and to see if there is any validity to the threat she made to you and your kind. But thanks to you and your running away like your ass was on fire, now I can't do the work that needs to be done. Instead I have to be here, babysitting you, making sure that you don't cause any more trouble."

"I don't need a babysitter. I'm old enough to take care of myself." Starling jumped in line for a taxi.

"You don't know what you need," he said. "Do you even have a place to stay? Or did you forget to plan that far ahead?"

She clenched her fist around the straps of her purse, which held her paperwork and wallet. "I have a plan. Thank you very much."

"Getting a taxi to the cheapest hotel isn't a plan." Jasper's eyes filled with fiery sparks as he stared at her.

"How did you know I was here?" she asked, hoping to divert his attention from her inadequacies.

"I'm allowed to have secrets."

"Well then, why don't you take your secrets and get moving. I need to take care of some business."

"And what business would that be?"

"If you know so much, then you don't need me to tell you." Starling stepped forward in the taxi line.

She hated being treated like she was stupid. Though she was just short of nineteen, she was not a child. In fact, she'd barely had a chance to be young, thanks to the spirits and ghosts who invaded her reality. She'd been forced to grow up a long time ago.

"Why do you have to be such a pain in the ass?"

She whirled on him at that remark, ready to let him have it. How dare he take that aggravated tone with her? But he just smiled. The grin was more suited to a mischievous child than to the man who had broken her heart. The humid air clung to her skin, but it wasn't the heat that made the warmth rise in her cheeks. "If you think you deserve anything more from me after the way you treated me, you have another think coming."

"Let me make it up to you." His smile retreated. "I booked us both rooms not far from here."

She thought of the meager amount of cash in her wallet, but she wasn't sure if she was ready to start forgiving Jasper just to get a free room. "No."

"Look, I know you're pissed. You have every right to be. But you can't get around Savannah without me. The Catharterians are clearly already gunning for you, and I don't think I could live with myself if I let you get hurt."

Chapter Two

Starling's room in the Bohemian Hotel looked out over the Savannah River as the muddy water rushed by in its push to reach the Atlantic. She was perched on the edge of the bed, looking out the window, scanning the distance.

"Are they still bothering you?" Jasper asked.

She didn't move.

"Starling?"

"Hmm?" she asked, her attention turning to him.

"Are the spirits still bothering you?"

"No," she said, pausing. "I'm doing good, really."

He might have believed her if everything about her, even the way she perched on the tips of her toes like she was ready to take flight, didn't say otherwise. Her black hair sparkled in the evening light, the color so rich it looked slightly red. For a second, he wondered if she looked red and blue when she shifted into her swan form. He could just imagine her shift. Her taking off her shirt exposing her milky, white skin; flesh begging to be touched … it had to be the same over her entire body, all the way to her nipples.

His response pressed hard against his zipper, and he forced himself to turn away. She was off-limits for a thousand reasons, but at the top of the list was the fact that it was his job to protect her. The young woman could be nothing more than another person the Sisterhood had enlisted him to save from harm. The worst thing he could possibly do was put her in danger of falling in love, not just with him, but anyone.

"Why did you come down here, Starling?" If she told him it was to follow some guy, it would be hard not to lose his mind. Then again, it would surprise him if she had come down here for some stupid reason like a guy. She seemed so much more mature than most women her age. He couldn't be sure whether it was the way she was raised, with a mother who'd had her fair share of problems, or whether it was because Starling was a nymph, but unlike most college age women, she didn't spend her time trying on jeans or flipping her hair while she texted away on her cell phone.

"I'm surprised you don't know. You seem to know everything," she answered.

"I wish I knew everything. It would make my job a hell of a lot easier."

"You mean it gets easier than being a shadow?"

He ignored her jibe. She was angry. She had earned the right, but he didn't have to give her the response she was gunning for. Nothing good would come of a fight.

"Are you still shifting into your swan form?"

"Not since my mother was killed."

"If it will make you feel better to go for a fly, I can keep you from getting hurt."

"Really? You are going to tell me that you care how I feel?" She gave him a look of disgust. "Why don't you just leave?"

"Look, I'll leave, but if you need me, I booked the next room." He pointed to the right. "Don't go anywhere without letting me know. Savannah isn't a great place for you to be running, or flying, alone."

"If I need a babysitter I'll let you know."

•••

Starling had spent the night staring out the window, watching the lights of steamboats and liners as they passed down the river. When she'd finally slipped into the lull of sleep, her dreams had been filled with images of her mother's spirit. Each time she tried to ask her mother, Carey, about the books, her spirit would fade from view, until finally Starling had given up and just sat in silence.

The morning sun stole through the window and filled the room with its light.

Starling ... Asclepius's wraithlike voice broke the silence of her sleep-fogged mind. *I'm waiting. I need your help.*

"Go away," she said aloud.

Starling... you must find the Libros Umbrarum. *We need you ... you must help us.*

"What do you think I'm doing? Do you really think I want to go on a wild goose chase through a city where I don't know anyone? Do you think I like being assaulted by you and your ... your ... " Her anger rose as she searched for the word she needed. What could she call a group of ghosts other than a pain in her ass? "Your friends?"

I have no friends.

"Thanks to you and your kind, neither do I. Can't you just leave me the hell alone?"

If you don't help me, you will die ...

"You can go fuck yourself."

The ghost's laughter echoed through her like she was nothing more than an empty vessel. *Get the books. They hold the answer. If you can't do it, we will find another, but don't think we will go willingly.*

Her heartbeat thundered in her ears as a wave of panic passed over her. It wasn't the first time she had been threatened by a spirit in her life, but in the last six months, the spirits had been growing angrier. "I'm not afraid of you."

Yes, you are.

"I don't need you breathing down my neck. Go the fuck away."

She unzipped her purse and grabbed her pill bottle with the GX 149. All she needed was one of the tablets Harper had prepared for her and the voices would stop, at least for now. She opened the orange bottle's lid and peered inside. There were less than two dozen pills left. Taking out a white, oblong tablet, she swallowed it down.

Her phone rang and Jasper's smiling face filled the screen. A wiggle of excitement crept up her spine as she moved to answer. There was something nice about having someone around who actually gave a shit, even if he was paid to do so. Besides Harper and Chance, there was no one else alive who seemed to give a crap.

"Hello?"

"Sleep well?" Jasper asked.

"Better than normal." She tried to sound annoyed, but she couldn't stop her excitement from spilling into her voice.

"You ready to get back to Vegas?"

"Absolutely not."

Jasper sighed. "Your dad and Harper were upset that you didn't tell them you were leaving."

"Maybe I should've told them, but they would have tried to stop me, and I'm not going back, at least not yet. I have work to do." Ever since she'd graduated from high school, she'd spent her days getting ready for this trip. The last thing she would do was go back the second she arrived.

"Are you going to tell me what exactly you are talking about?"

"If I do, you promise you won't tell a soul?"

There was a short pause on the other end of the line. "You aren't here to kill anyone, are you?"

She laughed. "No, that's your job. Remember?"

"Funny," he said, his voice steely. "Get ready. We're heading out at ten. I already got our plane tickets."

"I'm not going anywhere. And if you promise to not tell anyone my secret, maybe you can stay. I could use a little help—I can always use a hand with my laundry."

"You're hilarious," Jasper said drily. "I'll be over in a minute." The phone cut off and she sat it back down on the wooden nightstand.

She slipped on her clothes, feeling her future hanging in the balance. If he decided to help her, he couldn't assume that she owed him anything. If he helped, it had to be on his accord and regardless of the dangers. More than likely, getting the books would be easy. All she had to do was get down to the bank with the paperwork she had brought and everything would be taken care of—as long as they didn't look too deeply into the paperwork's authenticity.

Starling dug in her purse and pulled out the key ring she had looked at a thousand times. The safe deposit box's key slipped to the front of the ring, and she read the words inscribed on its brass surface: Do not duplicate. First National Bank, Savannah, GA.

Grabbing her smartphone, she tapped in the first letters and her regular search popped up. Maybe this time it would find something new, something she had missed. She hit enter. Lines of purple websites flipped onto the screen, each one reading: **Bank Officers Indicted for Multimillion Dollar Fraud.**

Clicking on the top find, she read through the page. At the bottom: Unclaimed safe deposit boxes will be held by the acquiring institution, The Savannah Bank. She clicked through until she found the directions to the bank from the hotel.

A sense of hope crept through her, but inadequacy and doubt followed close on hope's heels. The only thing left she hadn't tried was prayer.

She bowed her head.

My Goddess, Epione, please help me find success. I just need something, something to help me get rid of the guilt I feel and the spirits who threaten me.

There was a knock. Starling made her way over and opened the door. Jasper leaned against the side of the wall, his arms crossed over his chest like he'd been waiting for ten minutes rather than a few seconds. She couldn't help but notice a little splash of shaving cream at the corner of his freshly shaven jaw. She wanted to reach up and wipe away the bit of froth, but instead she did nothing. It was nice to see that even he, the shadow, was imperfect.

"So what are you up to?" he asked, barely moving a muscle. "Why would you run away from home to a place like Savannah?" He paused for a second. "This city is a spirit hotspot. Is that why you chose to come here?"

"If I had my way, I wouldn't have anything to do with spirits, in their hotspot or out of it." She grabbed her purse and phone and walked out of the room. "I came here because the spirits told me I had to. They've threatened that if I don't get some books from a safe deposit box, they will keep coming after me."

"Why didn't you tell someone you were being threatened?" Now there was a suggestion from someone who clearly had no contact with the spiritual world. "For starters, do you really think it would make anything better? No one can help me, so why should I complain? And what would I have told Harper or Chance? To get everything ready for this trip, I had to steal the safe deposit box keys from Harper. Then I had to forge the will and everything else the bank is going to need to get to the box. I don't need anyone else getting into trouble trying to help me. I'm tired of everyone around me getting hurt. I'm not willing to put you at risk either."

"Look, Starling, I'm here to keep you safe. That means if you need something, I'm in."

"I just need to get into the bank, get the books, and get a handle on the spirits. Then everything will be okay. I don't need you."

"You're not going alone."

"You may get hurt. I told you, I don't want anyone else to get hurt for me."

"Then tell yourself I'm putting myself at risk for the Sisterhood."

There was an inexplicable pain in her chest at his flippant response. "Fine."

"It's a damn good thing you're a nymph," he said, ignoring her shortness. "Or I would say you don't have a chance in hell of getting into the bank vault."

"What does being a nymph have to do with getting in?"

Jasper gave her a sideways glance. "Won't you use all your, you know, *feminine wiles*?" He shifted uncomfortably and stood up from his position against the wall.

She snorted with laughter. "Did you really just say feminine wiles? What are you, eighty?" She walked ahead, leading the way downstairs to the lobby.

The thought of using her power for seduction made her skin crawl. Yes, it was something she could turn on and off, not some innate attraction, but with this power came problems. The only time she'd used her gift had been on a poor neighbor boy when they were fourteen. She hadn't a clue what she was doing. She'd asked the kid to share his slice of pizza, and when he'd said "no," a strange energy had passed over her body. The next thing she knew, he was handing her the entire box.

He'd been hard to get rid of after that day. His affections led to his showing up at her door in the middle of the night, love letters, and playlists. He'd only stopped when his family finally moved away.

She didn't need any more stalkers. She already had more than her fair share of the dead kind.

"Where's this bank?"

She pulled her smartphone from her purse and tapped a few buttons. "It looks like it's only a few blocks from here." She slid her phone back into her purse. She looked up and caught him staring at her with his earthy brown eyes. At their center was a ring of blue, so faint that if she hadn't been in the right light, she would have missed the haunting, but sexy, mixture of colors. "I've been wondering, how old are you?"

She couldn't look away from the blue oasis in the desert of his eyes.

"Twenty-three."

A burst of energy surged up from her stomach, but she tried to ignore the feeling. She couldn't feel anything for this … shadow. "Seriously? Huh. I would have thought you were like, thirty."

"Thirty isn't old, you little shit."

"I didn't say it was. I just meant that you look older." She finally managed to divert her gaze. "And we're going to have to come up with some kind of backstory if you are going to keep tagging around with me."

"We'll cross that bridge when we get there, but I'm hoping, if everything goes right, we are going to be in and out of the bank and then back to your dad and Harper on the ten o'clock flight." Jasper opened the door leading to the parking lot and waited for Starling to pass through.

She stole another glance at his enchanting eyes as she passed by. "Here's hoping everything goes according to your plan."

Chapter Three

The entire bank smelled like industrial strength cleansers and bullshit. Over the last few years, since going to work for the International Legislative Organization of Nymphs who called themselves the Sisterhood, Jasper had gotten really good at identifying that pungent smell of people who lied for a living. Though admittedly, ever since Ariadne Papadakis had taken on the Sisterhood leadership role, life had been a little easier—at least when he'd had to deal with the leaders.

Starling weaved past him and headed for the row of tellers waiting to take people's money. There was only one man in the row of women, and Starling made a beeline toward him. "Excuse me?"

"Yes, ma'am, how may I help you?" the middle-aged man answered in a thick Georgian drawl.

"I need to get into my safe deposit box. It used to be housed at the First National Bank. I think it's now here?" Starling's voice wavered with nerves.

Jasper walked up behind her and put his hand on her lower back, appearing to comfort her. If she played it right, they would be in, out, and gone. He could go back to work trying to dig up facts about the Catharterians from the FBI files he had hacked into, and she could go back to the care of her family.

Soft warmth radiated from her where he'd placed his hand, and he pulled away. She definitely needed to get back to her family.

The older man glanced at him and smiled. "Not a problem, ma'am. Do you have your key?"

Starling rifled through her purse and pulled out a ring of mismatched keys. "Right here," she said, lifting a little brass key.

"Great," the man answered with a smile. "Let me take you to the bank manager."

If they left Georgia on the ten o'clock flight, they would be back to Vegas before midnight. As soon as he got back, he could work on finding the Catharterians' lair. He was so close to finding the location, he could almost taste it. Once he found their home base, he could get a population estimate. From there, he could figure out exactly how much danger Starling and the Sisterhood were in and how to protect them.

The man led them to an office where a black man sat behind a desk, typing away on his computer. "Devon, sir? We have a young lady here who needs to get into her safe deposit box."

"Thanks, Jim. I'll take care of her." Devon looked up from his work and smiled at Starling, but as he noticed Jasper, his expression faded and annoyance took its place. "Do you have your key?"

Starling jingled the ring. "Right here." She flashed Devon a flirtatious glance, one that Jasper recognized from their time in Vegas, one that made whispers of jealousy creep through him.

"Great," the man said. He stood up and straightened his suit jacket. The employee glanced up at Starling before his gaze wandered down to her chest and lingered a moment too long. "Just need to take care of a few things and you can get just what you need."

The man's words made the hairs on the back of Jasper's neck stand on end. "Yeah, we just need to take care of a few things before we get married."

"Married," the man said with a raised eyebrow. "Congratulations." He finally turned his gaze away from Starling. "I just love to see happy couples."

Starling shot Jasper a look, but he pretended not to notice. It had been her idea that they run under the cover of a relationship. It wasn't his fault if it was inconvenient.

"Follow me," Devon said, walking past them and out to the elevator. They waited in silence as the ancient elevator whirred and buzzed to a stop in front of them.

He hated elevators. People were too close. There were too many possibilities for attack. Not that the bank manager would attack. No. There was no bulge at his ankle or hip. He wasn't carrying a gun, but he had to weigh about two-fifty. In an enclosed space, Devon had the size, but Jasper had the experience.

The doors slid open. "Ladies first," Devon said, motioning for Starling to step through. Before Jasper could take a step, the manager shoved his way in next, making his percolating anger roil.

Jasper wedged his body between Starling and the man, and she shot him another sharp glance. "Small elevator, eh?"

Devon answered with a grunt and pushed the button for the lower floor. "Miss, I'm going to need your box number, your signature, and your key when we get down there. Then we can get out of these *small* elevators." He eyed Jasper.

"The less time we spend here, the better." Starling's elbow connected with the middle of his ribs, but he bit back a grimace of pain. "Lots of wedding plans to take care of. Isn't that right, honey?" he asked, forcing a smile.

The door to the elevator opened and Devon led the way out. When he was about ten steps ahead, Starling turned to Jasper and put her hand on his arm to stop him. "You. Stay. Here." She pointed to a spot outside of the elevator's doors.

"No. I'm not leaving you with that guy. No way."

"Look, I don't know the box number. I don't have a chance in hell of convincing him I know my shit if you're constantly acting like my over protective boyfriend. Just give me five minutes. If I'm not back with the box, then you have my permission to act out whatever macho fantasy thing you have going on in your head right now."

"I'm here to take care of you. If I let you walk into that room with a man I don't know, I might as well go back to the Sisterhood."

"Jasper, it's not like some bank manager is going to be gunning for me. Really. He is just some stranger at a bank. Big whoop. Now quit being so paranoid. I've got this. If nothing else, I can send my ghost friends after him, right?" She sent him a wilting smile, but it did little to quell his apprehension.

"Five minutes."

Starling turned. Devon stood at the end of the hall, waiting. "Not coming?" the manager asked with a wide smile that made Jasper want to punch his teeth down his throat.

"I'll be right out here."

Devon stuck out his arm for Starling to take. Starling looked over her shoulder and mouthed the words "Be good" before accepting it.

She was just lucky that Jasper wasn't the kind to kill out of jealousy.

He started to take a step after the couple but stopped. The bank manager wasn't a danger, only an annoyance. He couldn't act like this. He couldn't act like he cared.

• • •

Devon turned to the computer. "It says that the safe deposit box is located here after being moved from the First National Bank. What did you say the box number was?"

Starling smiled. "Well, the thing is that I don't actually know." She pulled the keys from her purse and laid them on the table. "But here is the key."

"The keys they used didn't come stamped with a vault number." He tapped a few keys. "What is your full name?"

"Starling Jackson, but the box is under the name Jenna Cygnini."

He looked up from the screen. "And you are Jenna?"

"Can I pretend that I am?" she asked, trying to use the most seductive voice that she could muster.

Devon's rich, chocolaty skin looked so soft, but his biceps pulled dangerously against the seams of his suit jacket as she moved in closer. She had told herself she wouldn't seduce a man to get what she wanted, but standing here now, staring at Devon's tiger-like eyes, it was hard not to give in to her whim.

He cleared his throat, and no matter how hard she tried, she couldn't seem to catch his gaze. "Are you saying that you are not the owner of the safe deposit box?"

"Not exactly. My aunt, Jenna Cygnini, passed away a few months ago. I'm just here to collect her things."

"Do you have her will stating that you are her benefactor?"

"Yep." Sweat started to collect in her palms as she reached into her purse and pulled out the folder she'd carefully put together over the last six months. "I think you will find all the documents you need inside."

Devon took the file folder and laid it out on the desk. He scanned over the will. She wiped her hands against the legs of her jeans, doing anything to calm her nerves.

He looked up, a frown on his face. "It says here that one Harper Cygnini is the will's benefactor."

"I know, but keep reading. It says that I'm supposed to get a collection of hers, a collection that resides in one of your safe deposit boxes." She glanced up at Devon, who was still frowning. In a desperate attempt, she bent over, making sure to squeeze her perky breasts so that they just peeked over the neckline of her v-cut shirt. "See," she said, pointing at the clause, "right here."

She could feel his gaze brush over her bare skin.

"I don't know about it," he said, but his voice was weak. One little sexy nudge and he would be in her pocket.

"I completely understand. But if you notice, all the other documents are in order. I have the probate court's signatures stating that I have submitted the will and they have approved for me to open the box." She pushed the will aside, so the probate court's order came into view. It was amazing what a person could get online.

She gathered the fake paperwork. "And here is Jenna's deed to her burial plot."

That had been a little tougher to gain access to. But now all Starling had to do was provide a fake signature. As long as he didn't look too closely, her ruse would work.

Devon glanced over the burial deed. He flipped the will back over. The sweat pooled in her palms and she wiped her hands over her jeans a second time. Chance would have been ashamed at her obvious tell, but hopefully the manager wasn't much of a poker player.

Devon pointed at the will. "I can't help but notice that there's no notary seal."

Crap.

"What?" she asked in a strangled voice. "That's weird. It came from our lawyer."

"Under normal circumstances, I wouldn't allow you access without first checking the authenticity." He picked up the papers and arranged them back in the file. "But if you make a deal with me, I would be willing to overlook any issues."

Starling's throat tightened. She was desperate to get into the safe deposit box, but was she willing to do anything? What if he asked her for sex?

Some prices were too high.

"What do you want?" she asked, her voice seductive but guarded.

"Before I ask, you need to tell me about your fiancé."

"Who?"

Devon's full lips pulled into a handsome but unnatural smile. "The man you came here with."

Double crap. How could she have forgotten about Jasper?

"He's not really your fiancé, is he?"

"What gave it away?"

Reaching over, he took her hand. "You aren't wearing a ring. I've learned that women love to show off their rings." Her fingers slid into his enormous palm, like he was a duke from one of her romance novels and he was asking her to dance. She'd never felt so much like a princess. Then again, she'd not had the full attention of a real man before—boys, yes, but never a man—except for her brief moment with Jasper in Vegas. "Is he even your boyfriend?"

She shook her head.

"I would love to go on a date with you, Miss Starling."

"Isn't that blackmail or fraud or something? Couldn't you get into trouble?" She stared down at her fingers. Her skin was milky and pale against his.

"Oh, we don't need to look at it like that, do we? Besides, it's not like your aunt is going to come after the bank for letting you into the safe deposit box. At least this way we both will get something we want."

She nibbled at her lip. Jasper was going to have a holy fit if she told him she had arranged for a date with the bank manager. It was a wonder he hadn't had a stroke in the elevator when he pushed his way in between them. He would never agree to her seeing Devon. Then again, she didn't need his permission.

"Okay. One date."

"Only one?" Devon's eyes sparked with devilishness. "I'll believe that when I see it."

"Not much of an ego, I see," Starling countered.

"No ego. I just know that after one night out with me, you will be begging for more."

Her laugh echoed out into the concrete halls. "No ego my ass."

Devon leaned to the side, his suit jacket pulling tightly, only further defining his well-toned muscles. "Oh, I would love to get another look at your ass all right."

She turned slightly, just to give her duke a glance of what he wanted. "One date. You have to prove to me that you're a gentleman."

He stood up straight and wiped the confident smile from his face. "If it's a gentleman you want, I'm your man. I know exactly how to treat a lady, Miss Starling."

"Safe deposit box first." She motioned toward the vault.

"Where are you staying?"

"The Bohemian."

"All right, the Bohemian at seven."

"While I'm looking through the safe deposit box, you can decide where we'll go this evening."

"Done." He clicked a few buttons on his computer screen and then, using a set of keys from his pocket, unlocked the vault. "I'll be waiting out here. When you're done, just knock on the door and I'll let you out. And take as long as you need. I'm going to need a while to plan something … unforgettable."

Chapter Four

The inner doors of the vault closed and Starling waited for the sound of the gates. After a second, the haunting clank of the metal closing filled the room, reverberating off the thousands of green metal boxes that lined the walls. On the table in front of her was a large, rectangular box. It sat unlocked but unopened.

What if the spirits had done nothing but led her on a dead-end journey? What if they had been wrong? She had spent almost all of her money getting down here and had only a small supply of her medication to keep away the spirits. Her only hope was that the *Libros Umbrarum* would be inside or she would have nothing left. No hope. No chance for recovering from her affliction. She would be left to the mercy of the dead.

Trying to rid herself of her nerves, she gave one long exhale. She'd come so far in her quest for the books, now wasn't the moment to be weak. The metal was cold and unyielding under her fingertips. The green box was the color of vomit, and merely the thought made her stomach turn.

Don't worry. The books will be inside. Don't worry. She repeated her mantra over and over in her head.

She lifted the lid.

The air in her lungs escaped in one long wheeze. Sitting in the bottom of the box was a lone, black feather.

The Catharterians had beaten her there.

• • •

He couldn't stand it any longer. She'd been inside the vault for too long. Jasper made his way down the hall from the elevator and stopped at the entrance to the small office that led to the safe deposit box area. Another minute and Jasper would break the gates down and go after Starling. The only thing stopping him was that asshat, Devon, working away at his computer, no doubt trying to make himself look busy so he wouldn't have to face the fact that Jasper stood just a few feet away.

Jasper clicked away on his phone as he looked through the emails the Sisterhood had sent him. He tapped nervously, the sound filling the small space as he attempted to think about anything other than Starling and all the things that could go wrong. He didn't trust Devon. Something about the asshat's face made his skin crawl. Sure, she was enclosed in a bank vault, but what if she wasn't really alone? What if a Catharterian was waiting for her? What if there was a fake exit?

He tried to quell his fears. It was just a bank. He was overreacting.

"Hey, man, can you keep it down?" Devon asked with a look of annoyance.

The floodgates opened at the sound of the asshat's voice, and Jasper shoved his phone back into his pocket. "Open the door," he ordered. "It's been long enough."

"Look, man. From the way you are acting, it's no wonder she wanted a little break."

"I'm allowed to worry. She's my fiancé," Jasper said, but he could feel his entire body twitch as he said the word. The first time it had been amusing, but something about repeating it made him uncomfortable.

"Funny," Devon answered, as he looked back down at his computer screen.

"What's so goddamned funny?"

"That you are still lying about your relationship with her. Starling told me the truth."

He imagined grabbing Devon by the throat and slamming his face into the computer's monitor.

"And to be honest," Devon continued, "she seemed more than happy to agree to go on a date with me."

"Bullshit." He focused on keeping his body still, anything to stop himself from lashing out at the prick.

"No bullshit, man." Devon stapled a stack of papers together and laid them on the desk. "My guess is that a guy like you couldn't do anything to please a woman as beautiful as her." He looked up. "It's a good thing she found me."

"If you don't shut the fuck up and stop calling me *man,* man, the only thing you're going to find is my foot in your ass."

"I see you're a sorry loser, *man.*" Devon looked up, a condescending sneer on his face. "What do you think you are going to do? There are security cameras everywhere here. If you lay one single finger on me, you will find your ass behind bars."

"Fuck you."

"What was I thinking? At least if you are behind bars, your little *fiancé* and I won't have to worry about you hovering over us." Devon leaned over forward. "What's your thing with her, anyway? If you're not her fiancé, what are you?"

"That's not any of your goddamned business. You don't need to worry about anything to do with her or us. You won't be seeing her again."

"Wanna make a bet?"

There was a tap from the other side of the doors. Devon stared him down as he walked over and unlocked the vault. Starling came into view; her black hair was disheveled and a few strands were stuck to the side of her face. Her eyes were red and bloodshot, there were no books in her hands, and her purse hung limply on her arm.

"Starling," Jasper said, racing to reach her before Devon even had the time to respond. "Are you okay? What was in the box?"

"I'm fine. They weren't there," she replied. "Let's just go." She passed Devon a weak smile.

"Are you okay?" Devon asked. "If you're not feeling well, we can postpone our dinner. I'd understand."

Jasper clenched his jaw. He didn't need a fight right now. First things first—he needed to get Starling back to the hotel. Then he needed to find out exactly what had been in the box that rattled her.

"It's going to be okay, Starling. We'll go pack up our stuff and catch the next flight out."

"No," she said, but she couldn't raise her gaze from the floor. "I have to find … " She glanced up at Devon and then back down at the floor. "I have to find what I need. Besides, I promised Devon I would go out with him. If nothing else, I'm good to my word."

He wanted to grab her by the shoulders and tell her exactly what a prick Devon was, but now wasn't the time—at least not in front of the banker. Jasper had the upper hand; all he had to do was get her out of the building and away from the creeper, and if he played his cards right, neither of them would have to see Devon again.

Chapter Five

When she'd left Vegas, Starling whole-heartedly believed that things would go her way. Everything in her life had been turned upside down in the last few months since she had been uprooted from her deceased mother's apartment and moved halfway across country with a father she barely knew and his new wife. It only seemed fair that the fates would eventually be on her side. What a naïve fool she had been. Why had she even bothered to hope? Life was never fair.

She buried her face into her pillow.

"Why did you agree to go on a date with Devon?" Jasper asked, pulling her attention away from her wallowing and back to him.

His face was a contorted mixture of anger and annoyance, but the way the lines collected around his lips made her wonder if he felt something else, something resembling jealousy. A wiggle of excitement rose from her belly at the possibility. "He noticed that my papers didn't have a notary's seal. I had to agree to the date or else I wouldn't have gotten in."

Jasper nodded and folded his hands together behind his back. "You don't intend on actually going, do you?"

"I don't have much, Jasper. The only thing I have is my word. It would be a shame to lose that."

Jasper stood quietly for a moment. There was no way he was going to talk her out of this. Devon was gorgeous from head to toe. Even the way he smiled screamed sexy. If nothing else, having him at her side would take her mind off the lost books.

She smiled for a second as she noticed the way Jasper's jeans clung to the arch of his ass. He bent forward and his shirt moved up, exposing the dimples just above his waistband. Excitement sprang up from the depths of her belly and then sank back down to deeper, more forbidden places.

"What exactly are these books you were looking for?"

She looked away from his perfect ass and tried to concentrate on something other than her growing need to feel a man's touch. "They're called the *Libros Umbrarum*. I don't know much about them other than the name means *Books of Shadows* in Latin, and the spirits keep pushing me toward them." She rolled onto her side. "Even Harper's sister, Jenna, wanted me to have the books. She left them to me in her will. I didn't even know they existed until she died."

"Why are the spirits hellbent on getting these books?"

"The spirits keep telling me they are the key to helping them 'cross over' and that they will help me gain control over the voices that I hear. I'm low on my supply of the GX 149, plus they are losing their effectiveness. The *Libros* are my only hope; if I don't do something I fear I'll go mad."

"Harper is close to making more, isn't she?"

"She was able to make a small batch before the company she used to work for found out she was using company equipment for a personal project on drugs—and to top it off, they somehow found out it was a drug that didn't pass FDA approval. She was fired. Now she's a year away from having her new lab up and running. By then I doubt they will have little effect on my control of the voices."

"I didn't realize …" Jasper turned. "So what can we do? Where are you planning on searching next?"

Starling sucked in a breath. "I have no idea. They were supposed to be in that bank, but I think the Catharterians beat me there. They must have them. First, they showed up at the airport and now a black feather in a secret bank vault? They're the only shifters who change into a vulture. They're the only ones who know about the drugs and would have access or the motivation to access our secrets. With the books in their hands, I won't be getting them any time soon."

"How much contact do you have with the spirits? Could they help you find your books?"

"They didn't even know the Catharterians had the *Libros*. I would doubt they have any clue where they put my books."

"But that's just the spirits you talk to on a regular basis. Do you think it's possible there are spirits out there you haven't met who could point us to the Catharterians' lair?" Jasper's eyes were bright with excitement, giving him the look of a kid talking about getting a Christmas present. He mustn't have learned the lesson of hoping for something that just wasn't going to happen.

"Spirits aren't easy to work with. They don't come when you want or need them. They only come to you when they want something. The dead are the worst kind of people."

Jasper's laughter echoed through the room.

"It's amazing what happens to a soul when their actions are no longer dictated by the laws of other people's judgment."

"So we can't go to selfish souls for help, is that what you're telling me?"

"No," Starling said, sitting up with excitement at the idea that just hit her. "*I* can't control spirits. But there are others who can. Maybe they can help us find the Catharterians." She slipped her feet into her Converses and made her way to the door. "You coming?"

"I guess we won't be flying anywhere today."

"At least not by plane." Some of her tiredness drained away as she smiled. There was still a glimmer of something that almost resembled hope.

* * *

The psychic's shop smelled like burnt sandalwood. The lights were low, drawing long shadows across the well-worn wood floor. A set of bells jingled as the door shut behind Jasper.

The store was filled with jars of dried rosebuds, purple thistles, and various collections of green herbs. On the wall across from Starling, shelves held candles, hand-carved boxes, wands, and an assortment of pentagrams. In the corner of the room was a doorway, covered in a purple cloth.

"It doesn't look like anyone's here. Let's go," he said, stepping back toward the door.

The curtain moved and a middle-aged woman stuck her head out. The woman smiled with her entire face as she glanced at Starling. "Hello, y'all. Welcome to the Goddess Shop. I'll be right with ya; just fixin' to finish up a spell. Feel free to take a look around." She disappeared behind the curtain.

Jasper pointed his thumb toward the door, but Starling shook her head. Maybe it was the rich scent of incense or the energy that buzzed through her, but something about this place felt like home.

She made her way to a collection of stones arranged in a clear glass box and idly ran her finger over a blue stone. It could have been her imagination, but a slight tingle of energy passed from the stone and up her finger. She drew her hand back. "What do you think they use all this stuff for?"

"I would guess witchcraft."

She glanced back at Jasper, who hadn't moved from his place by the door. "I know they're for witchcraft, but how do you think they use them?"

"How do I know? Maybe they throw them at each other."

There was a laugh from behind the purple curtain. "We ain't children. We find no need to pitch rocks at one another." The woman stepped out again. "Though I gotta admit there are more than a few people I'd like to wallop."

"So what do you use them for?" Starling asked, pointing to the collection of crystals, amethysts, onyx, and assortment of stones.

"Some believe that each stone carries with it a different property. Amethyst, that purple crystal there, is for reflectin' negative energy." She glanced over at Jasper. "If you're always with him, I don't think it would be such a bad thing to have on hand." She walked across the room, picked up a little crystal and, walking back, slipped it into Starling's hand. "On the house."

"I'm not always negative," Jasper grumbled. He opened his mouth to say something else but stopped.

"We shall see who you really are, I'm sure." The woman smiled, the light once again returning to her eyes. "By the way, I'm Jamie Blithe, daughter of the high priestess Tamsin Blithe. You may call me Jamie."

"Tamsin, as in Ariadne Papadakis's witch? She's your mother?" Starling asked, stumbling over her words.

Jamie smiled. "The one and only. As I've heard, she has done quite a bit for *your* kind."

Starling gripped the amethyst tighter, until the small crystal cut into the flesh of her palm. How did Jamie know? "We owe her so much."

"Oh no, I think she got her reward when she got to take down that louse of a governor, Stavros."

"She did so much … I hate to ask you for anything, but …"

"But what?"

"But, I just have so many questions."

"About being a nymph or about being a medium?" Jamie said, not beating around the bush.

"How did you know?" The blood rushed out of her face.

"I have my witchy ways, darlin'." Jamie paused. "So what are you needin' help with?"

Was this woman, this witch, her answer? Could Jamie make the spirits go away and the voices in her head stop? "The spirits … they won't stop asking me for help. I've been taking drugs."

Starling tapped her purse. "But I don't have much left. I need something—anything—to make the spirits stop."

"And?" Jamie ran her fingers over the edge of a shelf like she already knew what Starling was going to ask and was trying to avoid the question.

"And, I was thinking that maybe there was something you could do, something you could give me, or a spell that could make the spirits stop." Starling's words rushed from her like floodwaters during a storm. "They're driving me crazy, invading my dreams, taking control of my thoughts, and whispering threats for hours at a time. I can't take a shower without a spirit threatening me. I can't have a quiet moment with my family without a spirit telling me what to do. I can't function, and if I don't do something soon, they will take everything. They've already taken my mother, my friends. I can't lose my life to this."

"Now, darlin', you can't go on blaming the ghosts for killing your mother. As I heard it, that was those damned old vultures. They love death, those dirty beasts."

There was a shift, as if suddenly the weight of the world had been lifted off Starling's shoulders. Jamie knew everything. And she didn't think she was crazy, or demented, or weird like everyone else.

"Yeah, the vultures were behind it, but if it hadn't been for me and my ghosts, my mom wouldn't have gotten wrapped up in the drug business and drawn the attention of the vultures. It's all my fault," Starling replied, trying to keep her throat from being crushed by the emotional weight of her words.

"Having a gift is hardly your fault," Jamie said, as she unscrewed a lid on a jar of herbs and dipped her finger inside. "And that is exactly what you have—*a gift*. It's not something that has to be such a burden. Talkin' to spirits is just something you got to learn how to handle."

"That's what I've been trying to do."

"Hiding behind medications isn't learning how to handle your gift. In fact, I would say you are wasting it." She wiped her herb-covered finger on her dress.

"I …" Starling sucked in a long breath. She never thought of it as wasting her gift. She'd tried to talk to the ghosts. She'd done their bidding and taken down their notes. The only thing that they wanted, the books, she couldn't give them. "I don't want this … It's no gift. It's a curse."

"That's enough," Jasper said, stepping in between her and Jamie. "You don't need to come down on her. She doesn't need this. She's had enough pain in her life."

"I'm not trying to cause her pain. In fact, I'm trying to get her to understand what she has is power."

"Don't talk like I'm not here." Starling put her hand on his arm, retaking control of Jasper. "If there's a way you can help me *learn* how to deal with this, I'm all ears. I'll do anything you want me to do. All I want to do is be able to handle these people who invade my mind."

"Look, darlin', I'm not a medium. I'm a psychic. There's nothing I can do other than tell you that you have to believe there's a reason you have been chosen by the gods. It isn't always easy having gifts like ours, but you must act with grace, charity, and compassion. If you do this, the gods will favor you. They'll help you in anything you fix your mind to."

"I don't need gods, I need answers. What more can I do? I came all the way down here to help the spirits, and I failed. I tried. Nothing I ever do is good enough. Nothing I do ever helps. I just feel more lost each day."

"You're not lost. You are only just starting to find your way." Jamie paused. "If you fight, you may find what you seek. Don't give up, darlin'. You will find your way. Even if it's not the path you had in mind."

"Let's go," Jasper said, taking hold of Starling's hand.

"What you so desperately seek is not the only answer. It'll only bring your more of what you dread the most."

Starling stood there in stunned silence, trying to understand everything the witch was saying. The books couldn't possibly bring more of what she dreaded; she was already living in the sea of souls—what else was there left to fear?

Jasper squeezed her fingers. "Don't worry, Starling. We'll get the books, even if it kills me."

Chapter Six

"You didn't need to stand up for me back there. I was fine," Starling said as she slipped on her red high heels. "I mean, I appreciate you trying to protect me, but Jamie wasn't trying to scare me. She was just trying to help—even if she was going about it the wrong way." She stood and walked to the door.

"How do you know?" Jasper couldn't look away from her toned calves. He'd never noticed how athletic Starling was, but standing there in her red miniskirt and red heels, she was the flame and he the moth.

"Let's just say I have experience with people …"—she stared at him—"who go about helping in questionable ways."

"Hey," he said, trying to notice anything but the way her red dress rose to her mid-thigh, just inches away from flashing the world. He could almost feel the softness of her thighs as he imagined running his hands up her skin, lifting the dress, and taking what his body desired. He shifted in the chair. "You need to change. You can't see Devon looking like that."

"Who do you think you are?" she retorted, running her hands down her dress. "I just bought this dress. Just because you pretended, and failed, at being my fiancé doesn't mean you get to have an opinion on what I wear or who I wear it for."

Who she wore it for. Maybe that was what really bothered him. He hated that asshat Devon. If Jasper had his way, she would wear that dress only for him.

"I'm going to say it again: I don't like this. I don't think you have any business going out with him."

"You've already made that more than clear, but you don't have a valid argument for why you hate him so much." She grabbed her purse. "Just because he is interested in me doesn't mean you should care. I mean, you don't *like* me. You left me for the last few months. Now you don't get to be possessive."

"I left because I had to."

Her high heels clicked on the hardwood floor as she walked to the hotel room's door and opened it. "Well, now I *have* to go. And who knows? Maybe Devon won't leave."

She shut the door. He waited for a minute and followed her out, careful to stay enough distance behind her so that she wouldn't know he had followed.

Didn't Starling understand that he cared about her? That he wanted her? But she was someone he could never have.

He stopped in the middle of the lobby as Starling slid into the backseat of the town car where Devon must have been waiting. Her face lit up with a smile as the driver closed the door.

A strange knot formed in his stomach. Her face never lit up like that for him. Maybe she never really cared about him. Hell, if she did there would have been a glimpse of something, some attraction underneath her anger. Yet, there had been nothing, only the annoyance.

He was the real asshat for wanting her.

Jasper waved for a taxi, and getting in, gave the man directions to follow the black town car. The driver answered with a grunt and pulled behind Starling and Devon's car. He hated this. Why couldn't they just get along, find the books, and get back to Vegas? Then again, as soon as they returned to Vegas, he would go back to investigating the Catharterians. What a cluster fuck the investigation had become. Over the last few months he'd been working his ass off, trying to hunt down any leads about their identities and their organization. The latest lead he had was a man who claimed to be a vulture-shifter living in the Arizona desert.

As far as he could tell, their population was low, probably no more than fifty in the entire world, but it was hard to pin down an exact estimate. Aside from Dr. Redbird, the woman who'd killed

Starling's mother, he'd only come across the man in Arizona as a confirmed vulture. Every other lead he'd tracked down was either crazy humans or others who had been mistakenly identified as Catharterians. If he could just get his hands on the man, maybe he could get the answers he needed.

The only thing he knew with any certainty was what Dr. Redbird had told him: that the shifters needed to breed, and in order to breed, they needed Starling and her drugs. They had been more than willing to kill to accomplish their goals. They wouldn't stop in their pursuit.

Since he had chosen personal security as his career two years ago, he had learned one important lesson: an enemy who possessed secrets was an enemy who was one step away from succeeding. And he couldn't let them get their hands on Starling.

The car turned to the right and pulled to a stop in front of a piano bar called Banging Keys. Jasper smirked as he imagined banging Devon's face into a piano's ivories. The thought was so real it made his fingers twitch. The bar's brick exterior was worn with age, and its windows lined with velvet curtains that blocked unwelcome passersby from spying on the patrons. Devon had seemed so egocentric that a hole-in-the-wall piano bar was a far cry from the over-the-top haute cuisine restaurant where Jasper had expected him to take Starling.

Her red dress rose dangerously up her thigh as she stepped out of the town car. Devon walked around and waited until she wrapped her arm around his like they were attending some high school prom rather than a night out at some dingy club.

Handing the taxi driver a fifty, Jasper got out. But as he approached the door to the bar, the bouncer stuck out his arm and stopped him. "ID?"

"Really?" Jasper asked, digging in his back pocket for his wallet. It had been years since he'd been carded.

"Really." The guard crossed his steroid-enhanced arms over his chest, making his man boobs look even more pronounced.

Jasper flashed his driver's license to the bouncer. The bouncer took a quick look. "You can't come in."

"Ah, I get it," Jasper said, fishing out a hundred dollar bill from his wallet. "Here," he said, stuffing the money into the gorilla's hand.

The man wadded the bill into his palm, making it disappear. "Thanks for the tip. If you hurry you can still catch your taxi." He motioned toward the cab with his chin.

"What in the hell?"

The man stepped in front of the door and looked past him like Jasper wasn't even there.

So much for the hundred bucks.

"And fuck you, too," he growled, turning away from the impenetrable wall of man. As he moved to the taxi, the cell phone in his pocket vibrated with life.

"Hello?"

"Jasper?" a woman asked.

"You got him. Who's this?"

"This is Ariadne. I'm calling to check on the status of your investigation. It's come to my attention that you are currently in Savannah, correct?"

Word traveled fast, even to the Sisterhood on the other side of the world.

"I'm disappointed that you didn't think to notify us about the change in Starling's status. You know she's in danger."

"I'm aware, ma'am. That is why I followed her down here. I've been trying to get her to return to Vegas, but let's just say she's been less than accommodating." He looked back at the bouncer who stood between him and Starling. He had to get in. He would just have to find another way.

"Is she currently safe and out of the hands of our enemies?"

He tensed. "Absolutely. I have everything under control." He hoped he wasn't lying. He walked toward the taxi and got into the backseat. "One block to the right and stop." he said to the driver.

"What was that?" Ariadne answered.

"Nothing, we're just finding our way."

"Glad to hear it," Ariadne continued. "You need to find a safe place. We have reason to believe the Catharterians are growing in strength and have made Savannah their central location. Where exactly, we aren't sure. All I know with any certainty is that is the last place you and Starling should be."

"Floor it," Jasper said to the driver.

The man stepped on the gas, pressing Jasper into the backseat.

"Have you learned anything else?"

"All we know for sure is that they have set up a headquarters somewhere in Savannah. What they are trying to do, aside from getting their hands on the formula, or Starling and her supply, is hard to say." There was a long pause on the other end of the line. "They are growing more frantic. They lost another of their kind at our hands this week. There's a war coming and we all need to be ready."

"What happened?"

"We had an attack here in Crete. They tried to come after our other young nymph, Trina. Luckily, her fiancé, Kaden, came in and made short work of the vulture. We found out the vulture was working for some kind of faction within the Catharterians, but not much else," Ariadne paused. "Needless to say, we've put Trina in protective custody until this is over, and the vultures are no longer a threat. I can't stress how much danger Starling is in. You need to get her somewhere that no one can find her."

"We'll be back to Vegas on this evening's flight."

"Good. It's a start. At least in Vegas she'll have the hotel's security and yourself. Keeping her safe is about to get a lot harder."

He cringed. It was already a challenge keeping a headstrong girl who wouldn't listen to reason out of trouble. The last thing they needed was to stay in the Catharterians' home field.

"I have everything under control."

There was a pause. "That's what you said last time …"

He clenched the phone. "I won't make the same mistakes."

"You better not. There's too much at stake." The line cut off.

The cabby pulled the car to a stop just short of the back door of the club. He handed the man more money and got out. "Park around front. If things keep going my way, I may need you again."

"You got it, boss," the cabby said as he stuffed Jasper's money into his pocket.

Two waiters were standing outside, smoking cigarettes and laughing about some joke Jasper had missed. He made his way over, making sure to stick to the shadows that ran deep down the back road. The back of the bar stunk of garbage, liquor, and sickness, and it was hard to sit behind the dumpsters, but thankfully he didn't have to wait long for the men to snuff their cigarettes and go inside. He darted to the back entrance, and with a quick glance around for another muscled bouncer, he snuck inside.

A man sat at a piano perched in the middle of the stage. He played a slow, bluesy version of the song *Rock Me Baby*. Jasper couldn't help but step in beat with the catchy song as he made his way toward the main room of the bar. He'd always loved blues; too bad he and Starling couldn't have been here under different circumstances.

Sitting in the corner in the VIP section were Devon and Starling. Devon had pulled her chair close to his, and he had his arm draped across the back. He leaned in and said something into Starling's ear, and she started to laugh. Her sound was masked by the pianist's song, but just seeing her this happy made Jasper want to sprint across the bar and enact his fantasy of pushing Devon's face into the piano. On the other hand, it was nice to see her having fun, laughing. In truth, she probably needed a night out like this. No worries. No stress. No spirits.

• • •

Devon leaned closer, his Scotch-scented breath wetting her neck. "I just knew you would love the blues. This is one of my favorite places. Come here all the time."

"With your other dates?" Starling raised an eyebrow.

He leaned back as he answered with a full belly laugh. "You aren't jealous, are you? I thought you left that emotion up to your little lap dog, Jasper."

"Jasper isn't my lap dog. He's barely even my friend."

"Then why does he follow you around? Is he your brother or something?"

She fiddled with the end of her dress, pulling it down to cover more of her naked flesh. It was wrong to have come here. The more she got to know Devon, the more she wished she had stayed in her room. At least from there she could have spent her time trying to find out where the books were instead of being stuck on a date where she wanted nothing more than to shove a fork in the side of the man's neck. Maybe Jasper had been right.

"No, he's not my brother. He's my bodyguard."

"Your bodyguard?" Lines collected around the corners of Devon's eyes as he frowned. "Why would you need a bodyguard? Are you a foreign dignitary? A princess from Sweden? Oh god, the guys at the bank are going to love this!"

Of course, all he would care about was his image. "Yeah, I'm a princess from Sweden. Starling isn't my real name. It's really Asa, but don't tell anyone. Okay?" She held back the urge to roll her eyes at the banker's stupidity.

He's not as stupid as you think, a spectral man whispered.

She gasped at the sound of Asclepius's ghostly voice. Not here.

Then where? After your enemies kill you?

Starling clenched her eyes. Go away.

Trust me. You want me with you. I can help you.

Opening her eyes, Starling stood up. Devon took a long swig from his aged Scotch and gave her a sickening wink. "Where're you going?"

"I need to use the bathroom. Be right back." She started to walk away.

"If you need a hand in there, I'm your man!" Devon drunkenly called after her. Several of the people sitting around them stared at her, making her cheeks warm. *He's a wolf in sheep's clothing,* Asclepius said.

Shut up.

There was only one woman in the women's bathroom, and the blonde barely looked up as Starling walked in and closed herself in a stall. She sat down on the commode and opened her purse. Rifling through, she found the familiar orange bottle and took out a tablet. Her medication would make it all better. The pill stuck in her throat, but she forced the dry medicine down.

That will only keep me and my kind away for so long. We will keep coming until you get the books.

"Just shut up," Starling said, her voice echoing through the almost empty bathroom.

"Excuse me?" the woman at the sinks answered.

Starling dropped her forehead into her hands. I'm trying. I don't need you to keep pushing. I need the books, too. She paused mid-thought. Why do you need them? You're dead. It's not like you're reading.

We all need help. You cannot help us until you have reached your full potential.

Can't I help you without the damned books? What happens if I never find them? What if they're just gone?

You must find them.

Starling sighed. She didn't even know where to start. A black feather was the only clue—from there she had nothing, no direction to turn. *Where do I go from here?*

You leave this place. Go back to Jasper. He will lead you in the direction you need to go.

The only place he wants to go is back to Vegas and he will leave me again. How can I convince him to keep searching?

Tell him the ghost Asclepius has commanded you. And tell him that forgiveness can be found in moments of selflessness.

Starling sat up and ran her fingers over her hair. *Why should I trust you? You told me I would die if I didn't get the books. Why are you trying to help me all of a sudden?*

Let's just say there aren't many who are like you. True mediums are hard to find. Especially ones with your… qualifications.

Are you saying you need me? Starling smiled.

And you need me. As the drugs began to soak into her system, Asclepius's voice grew quieter. *Go back to Jasper. Trust him.*

She made her way back out to the bar. Her date had a fresh glass of Scotch sitting in front of him as she sat down. "Devon?"

"I hope everything went all right; you were in there for a while," he answered.

"I'm having a great time and all, but—"

"Hey, while you were in there some lady came by our table. Said she was looking for you," Devon said, interrupting. "She gave me this to give to you." He handed her a sealed envelope. Nothing was written on the outside.

"Did she say who she was?"

Devon shook his head. "She was good-looking but not as pretty as you." He tipped his glass toward her. "And she talked with an accent. Couldn't put my finger on where exactly it was from though."

Who would have tracked her down in a seedy out-of-the-way bar in a city where no one but Jasper knew where she was? Had he told someone where she was? Or, whoever had left her the letter must have been a supernatural, and whatever news the letter carried could only be more supernatural shit—shit she was trying to avoid. She ripped open the top of the envelope and pulled out the paper that was tucked inside. It read:

My dear Starling,

What you seek can be found where many ghosts wander. This magical place is where new memories are made and the moss whispers of the memories of the past. It is not round, but what lies at its heart is. Take a moment to remember and soak in the energy, and you may soon find your way.

Best of Luck

There was no signature.

Who would have written this cryptic note? And why? The only person besides herself who knew of her quest to retrieve the books was Jasper. Anger steamed through her. He had promised to keep her secret.

Asclepius had told her to return to Jasper, but how could she trust a man who might have betrayed her?

Chapter Seven

Jasper hoped to grab Starling as she'd left the restroom, but he stopped himself when he noticed the angry look in her eyes. Maybe the date wasn't such a success.

At Devon's table, the drunken fool slobbered over Starling, making Jasper's skin crawl. Up until a few minutes ago, he'd been hoping she had merely showed up to follow through on her word. Yet, as he watched Devon's hands roam the hills and valleys of her body, he couldn't deny that she must have been at least a bit attracted to the asshat.

He should have grabbed her when he'd had his chance.

He sat his glass down on the bar. Well, if she wanted to be with the banker, so be it. "Another round," Jasper said to the barkeeper, pointing at his drained pint.

"IPA?" the bartender asked.

He nodded. Beer would take the edge off his confusing mess of emotions.

The man slid the glass down the bar to him and took his money.

Devon leaned into Starling and ran his frog-like lips up her neck and over her chin. It was more than he could take. Grabbing his glass, Jasper rolled out of the shadowy corner and across the bar. He couldn't stand by idly and watch. Sometimes safeguarding meant having to protect a person from herself.

"You ready to go?" Jasper asked, interrupting the make-out session.

Starling jerked, away from Devon's slavering kiss. She wiped the back of her hand over her lips. "What are you doing here, Jasper?"

"I'm taking you back to the hotel. You need your rest." He bit his tongue to stop himself from saying what was really on his mind.

"You can take the hotel and shove it up your ass. I'm not some weak, fragile girl who needs a babysitter," she said, glaring at him. "I'm just fine here with Devon."

Devon looped his arm around her waist and pulled her closer. "That's right, baby, I got you."

"You can't be serious," Jasper said, motioning toward Devon. "This guy is the biggest asshole I've ever met. You don't need to slobber all over him just to make me jealous. I don't give a damn."

Starling leaned back, forcing Devon to loosen his grasp. "Did it ever cross your mind that maybe I don't care about you?"

"Come on now, Starling. You can lie about a lot of things, but you can't tell me you don't think of me at least as a friend."

"A *friend*," she spat the word, "wouldn't throw another friend under the bus the first chance he got. A *friend* wouldn't blab a secret."

"What in the hell are you talking about?" All he'd ever done for this girl was give, give, give. He'd voluntarily given up almost the entire last year of his life taking care of her and watching out for her. Hell, if put in a bad spot, he'd have taken a bullet for her. And now she was going to accuse him of being incapable of keeping a secret?

"I told you something … something you promised to not tell anyone …" She glanced at Devon. "And then I was given this." She thrust an envelope into Jasper's hand.

Taking out the note, he read the words. "Who in the hell gave you this?"

"I did," Devon growled. "Some chick gave it to me, told me to give it to Starling. I thought it was her friend or something."

"We aren't from here. We know no one. What makes you think the woman was Starling's friend? You didn't think to ask who she was?" Jasper's fingers tightened around the paper until it crunched in his hand.

"Hey, I'm not the one who is supposed to be her bodyguard," Devon said, twisting the knife.

"What exactly did you tell him?" he demanded of Starling.

Don't get angry at me. You are the one who told someone my secret."

"I didn't tell anyone anything. I've been following you around and trying, once again, to keep you from getting your ass in trouble."

"You haven't talked to anyone?"

"I don't know anyone here, and the only person I've spoken to other than you is the cabby who brought me here." But that wasn't entirely true. There was the phone call with Ariadne. He couldn't remember telling her anything that would have compromised the promise he made to Starling. Was it possible Ariadne sent the messenger? She knew about Starling's ability to speak to the dead, but she couldn't possibly have known about the secret books. Yet, someone out there knew. Someone who wanted to help. But why?

He had a hard time believing it was just for Starling. Maybe he was a cynic, but nobody helped someone else without some kind of selfish motive. They needed to get out of Savannah before anyone else came out of the woodwork. It seemed like every passing minute Starling fell further into danger.

"Why don't you get the hell out of here?" Devon drunkenly motioned toward the door. "She clearly doesn't need a shitty bodyguard. What she really needs is a good time and frankly, man, you're ruining it."

"Shut up, Devon." Starling pried herself loose from his grasp and stood up. "I couldn't have a good time with you even if you vibrated."

• • •

"Let me see the letter again," Jasper said. He read through it one more time. "Cabby, what's the best place here in Savannah?"

"What, sir?" the cabby asked, looking back at them.

"What would you say is a place where memories are made?" he tried again.

"I don't know about memories, but Savannah is known as the city of parks and squares. And Forsyth Park is a real popular place for weddings," the cabby answered, but his voice made it sound like more of a question.

"Is there something round there?" Starling asked, breaking the tense silent treatment she had been giving ever since they had left Devon alone at the bar. Jasper handed back her letter, and folding it, she put it back into her purse.

"There's a pretty nice fountain at its center. I guess that would be round," the cabby continued.

"Take us there," Starling ordered.

The cabby looked toward Jasper and he gave the man a nod.

"All right," the cabby said, turning to the wheel.

"You really didn't tell anyone what I told you?" Starling finally looked at him; the anger in her eyes had been replaced by a look of pain.

"No. I really didn't tell anyone."

Starling nodded.

"I'm glad you weren't really into Devon," Jasper said, trying to find anything to say that could keep her talking to him. "Tell me the truth. Did you go out with him just to piss me off?"

She looked away, but not before he noticed a smile flicker over her lips.

A wave of excitement shot through him, making him smile. "So you did?"

"I did no such thing." Starling's voice was flecked with laughter. "I told you, I went out with him because I made a deal. I'm nothing if not good to my word."

She couldn't have been more wrong. She had so much to give. Starling was smart, stubborn, headstrong, and unarguably one of the sexiest women he had ever had the chance to work with. Yet, he couldn't tell her what he really thought. They were already crossing the line between a professional relationship and something more; he didn't need to push things any further.

"You never told me what you found in the vault."

"The books weren't there," Starling said, shifting uncomfortably in her seat.

"But?"

"But what?" she asked, clearly avoiding his question.

"There was something else in the box, wasn't there?"

She reached into her purse and pulled out a black feather. "There was only this. I think it was a threat. I think the Catharterians may have taken the books and left me this." She spun the feather around. "They know my weakness. They know that if they pull one of my hairs, or take a feather when I shape-shift, I can be killed."

"Son of a bitch." Jasper took the feather and turned it in his fingers. The feather was so black and rich that it reminded him of Starling's long hair. He ran his finger down the barbs, letting them come apart under his touch. "When you were inside I got a call. The Sisterhood. Apparently, they think we're in a Catharterian hot bed."

"Huh? What do you mean?"

"Ariadne said they have reason to believe that Savannah is the headquarters of their leadership. Before they get to you again, we need to get these books and get out."

"If we leave, would we go back to Vegas?"

"Trina and Kaden have gone into hiding. I think that would be a good idea for you, too."

"You really want me to go into hiding?" Starling sat up straighter, readying herself for a fight.

"I just want to keep you safe. You know that. If that means that you have to go to Vegas, or Crete, or wherever, so be it. I just can't have you getting hurt."

Her shoulder drooped and she slumped in the seat. "Let's just worry about getting the books. Once we do, I promise I'll do whatever or go wherever you want."

Her reaction surprised him. She'd fought him every step of the way, and now she was resigning herself to the fact that she would be tucked away from the world until the Sisterhood's enemies were under control. It seemed so unlike her.

The car pulled to a stop at the north end of a large tree-filled park, and Starling hopped out onto the curb.

"Wait here," Jasper said to the cabby.

He followed Starling as she strode down the sidewalk toward a fenced large, white, Parisian-style fountain that sat at the center of the north end. A statue of a classic woman was perched at the top. She held her dress at her knee, but the iron skirt flowed as if a light breeze could flex the metal in which she was cast. The woman held a staff in her hand, in a way reminding him of the frescoes he had seen of Epione when he'd been in Crete with Ariadne.

Starling walked around the fountain, running her fingers over the black fence that surrounded it. After making a full circle, she sat down on a waiting bench. She dropped her head into her hands.

"What's wrong?"

"The books aren't here." Her shoulders trembled. "I'm never going to find them. I'm never going to be able to stop the voices or protect my mind."

He sat down next to her and took her hand. "There are other answers, Starling. We just need to look harder."

Uncertain of what he could say to make her feel better, he sat in silence and stroked the back of her hand with his thumb. The trickling water and the sounds of kids playing filled the air as Jasper watched the water spray. At the bottom of the fountain were four half-man, half-fish—Tritons—and in between them were four swans. Their white beaks were open, letting the water shoot upward, filling the air with mist.

"Take a moment to remember …" Jasper quoted the line from the mysterious letter. "What is there to remember here?"

"I don't know," Starling said as she looked up. She dabbed away the tears that rested on her cheeks. "Why didn't the person who sent us the letter just tell us where to go? And if they have the books, why didn't they just give them to me? Why does everything have to be so goddamned hard?"

Jasper smiled, masking his pity. No matter how tough she acted sometimes, she was young. So many tough moments were going to come her way. His stomach lurched—tough moments like the secret he had to keep from Starling about his past.

"Life is hard, Starling. It never gets easier." He looked down at their entwined hands. "I've learned that the moment you think you are okay is the moment that everything goes wrong. At least for you, and this quest, there's nowhere to go but up."

"That's fucked up. You know that, right?" Starling smiled, but there were still tears in her eyes.

His laughter spread out into the evening air. "Maybe you're right. I guess I'm a little fucked up."

In more ways than one.

She slid closer to him on the bench and lifting his arm, put it around her. He moved to take it away, but she held it against her body. Everything in him told him to pull away, that they were too close. That he was putting not only her, but everything in danger.

"I'm sorry about going after Devon." She leaned her head against his chest, as if she was trying to listen to his heart. If she could hear it, he had no doubt she would have been able to guess how nervous she and her little red dress made him.

"It's fine. It shouldn't have mattered." Jasper reached up with his free hand and moved a strand of her hair out of his face.

"But it did. I know it bothered you."

"Did you see the swans?" Jasper asked, trying anything to get away from the subject.

Starling laughed. "You don't have to act all tough all the time. I know you like me."

"I … I do like you, Starling. But you have to know it's only as a friend. Nothing more."

She nodded. "Right now, I'm happy to have that."

The water trickle filled the tense silence between them. He tried to measure the time by counting her breaths. In and out. Her body warmed against his, creating a layer of wetness between them, but he didn't mind. Something about holding her like this, her body against his, just felt right. Almost as if he could make amends for his mistakes by being here for her in her lowest moment.

"Starling, I need to tell you the truth about something …"

"Excuse me?" a woman behind them asked, interrupting.

Starling pulled away as Jasper turned. "Yes?"

Standing behind them, in a long white sundress, was a woman whose face was familiar and, as she smiled, a faint glow seeped from her skin and enveloped him, making his heart slow and making him feel as if he didn't have a care in the world.

"Hello, love," the woman said, her voice soft and melodic, like a bird's song. "I'm Epione."

"Epione?" Starling said, stunned. "What're you doing here?"

"You need me …"

"Can you make the ghosts stop?" Starling asked, her voice cracking with emotion.

Epione stepped closer and rested her hand on Starling's shoulder. "No matter what you do, the spirits of those who have passed will never leave you. You need to come to terms with your gift. You may not like it now, but with time, I know you will come to see the value in having those from the past in your life."

"I just want them to stop … I can't do this anymore."

Epione ran her hand over Starling's forehead, down her cheek, and lifted her chin like a mother to a child. "Sometimes the best gift we can give ourselves is a change of perspective. You are a strong woman. You have a strong heart and a strong mind. Sometimes it works against you." Epione let go of her chin and rested her hand lovingly again on Starling's shoulder. "Until you find the books, you must change your thoughts and think of what a wonderful gift you have been given instead of how hard your life has become. Remember, things could be worse."

"I know," Starling said.

"And remember, you have Jasper." Epione glanced over at him. "He may be as soft as a porcupine sometimes, but he is here because he has chosen to be. You must consider it an honor that he has chosen to give his friendship and alliance."

Starling sent him a soft, appreciative smile. "He can be a porcupine."

Epione's laughter whispered through the trees.

"What should we do next? Do you know where we can find the books?" Jasper asked, annoyed and wanting to get down to business while they had the goddess's attention.

Epione's smile disappeared. "After Starling prayed to me for help, I've been trying to locate the books."

"Have you had any luck?" He couldn't help his growing excitement. With the goddess's help, they would be out of Savannah and out of danger in no time.

"Unfortunately, I have."

"Unfortunately?" he asked.

"Well, I have found a clue. I've been told Gracie knows exactly where they may be located. However, she resides in a place I cannot enter."

He had never heard of such a thing. In fact, it was almost comical to think that a goddess would be unable to travel wherever her heart desired.

"Where can't you go?"

Epione's already pale face blanched. "Bonaventure Cemetery."

Chapter Eight

The Bonaventure Cemetery sat just outside of Savannah, and the cabby chatted away with Starling and Jasper as they made their way through the Spanish moss-cradled city. For the first time since she had arrived, Starling noticed the smell of swamp and hot boiled peanuts, and even more prominently, the rich scent of late-evening flowers. What kind, Starling couldn't be sure, but the floral fragrance was heady, almost intoxicating.

The cabby stopped at a crosswalk for a man in his mid-sixties who stood waiting by the light. The man walked across the street, staring at them as he made his way. His gaze slid over her like an icy wind, making goose bumps rise on her arms.

"Do you see that guy?"

Jasper looked out at the window at the man. "What about him?"

"He gives me the creeps."

The man turned his back to them as he stepped up on the curb.

Jasper frowned. "You want me to check him out?"

"No," Starling said, shaking her head. She was only imagining dangers, making up for her mistake in not seeing the threat that was Devon.

"You sure?"

She nodded.

Jasper eyed her for a moment and then turned to the cabby. "Do you know where we can find a lady named Gracie?"

The man glanced back at them in his rearview mirror. "What're you doing? Trying to fit every tourist spot into one day, sir?"

"Yeah, you know how it is," Jasper said, but his attempt at sounding nonchalant fell flat. "Is Gracie a tour guide at the cemetery?"

"Almost, but not quite." The cabby laughed. "Gracie is one of Savannah's resident ghosts. She's a little girl who was buried in the cemetery in the 1800s. Pretty little thing if you take a look at her statue."

"She's dead?" Starling shouldn't have been surprised. Of course Epione would have sent her to visit another member of the dead club.

"Yeah, some say that if you put something in her hand, the next day the item will be gone. Others have told of her crying if you take away what you have given her. So many people were trying to play with the little girl that they had to build a wrought iron fence around the little thing to protect her from being destroyed." The cabby turned down a street and slowly came to a stop in front of the main gates of the cemetery. "If you ask me, they should have left well enough alone. I bet the little thing is lonely now that no one comes to play."

The driver pulled into a parking spot behind a black SUV that looked eerily similar to the one she had seen pull away after the thief had tried to steal her bag at the airport. A man in a suit was standing on the sidewalk beside the car, talking on his cell phone. As the man noticed them, he turned away, but Starling didn't miss the fact that he continued watching them from the car's side view mirror.

After a few moments, he walked around to the driver's side to get into his car, but not before his green eyes caught her gaze and he sent her a bone-chilling grin. He got in and the car quickly pulled away.

She opened her mouth to tell Jasper about her suspicion the Catharterians were tailing them, but she stopped. She couldn't be sure it was the same man or even the same car model as the one that had been parked outside of baggage claim. She was just being neurotic since being attacked. She needed to stay strong.

The cemetery entrance was just a few steps from the cab. Starling could already sense the sad energy that filled the place. "Where's her grave?" She hated to spend any more time here than necessary. The last time she'd been in a cemetery was for her mother's funeral, and as she peered out the window at the long rows of grave markers, memories of her funeral possession made a sick feeling rise in her stomach.

"It's in Section E. It's something you won't soon forget," the cabby replied.

"Got it," Jasper said with a nod. "You mind sticking around a little while longer? I think we'll need a ride back to the hotel and then the airport when we are through here. Okay?"

"Not a problem, sir. I got no better place to be on this fine summer evening." The cabby put the car into park. "I'll wait right here if you got any more questions, sir."

Starling got out of the car and the sad, humidity-cooled air draped over her shoulders like a shroud.

"You ready?" Jasper asked, stopping beside her.

She nodded. She was as ready as she was going to be.

Jasper took her hand and led her through the gates. A few couples milled about, but for the most part, the place was almost empty, and their only psychical company was hundreds of tombstones. Some of the markers were covered with figures of angels, statues of Jesus, and markings that Starling didn't recognize. If it hadn't been for the blanket of sadness, it would have been easy to be swept away by its ethereal beauty. *You shouldn't be here,* a female ghost whispered as they neared a mausoleum. The house-like structure was made of white and gray marble with a cobweb-covered stained glass window at its entrance.

Starling moved closer to Jasper, trying to not pay attention to the new, unwelcome voice.

This is no place for you, a different woman's voice repeated the ominous warning.

You will find only death in this place, a male ghost whispered.

It had been less than two hours since her last dose of medication, but it didn't stop her from reaching in her purse and getting another pill.

"You okay?" Jasper asked as she dropped the bottle back into her purse.

Starling nodded. She should have expected to be inundated by spirits in a cemetery. The last time she had been able to rely on her medication crutch to make it through the bustling crowds of the dead. But this time, with the drugs not working as well as they had, she was on her own.

Jasper pulled her closer. "It'll be okay. I got you."

Maybe she wasn't as alone as she felt, but there was little he could do to protect her from the spirits.

She glanced down at the plaque on the mausoleum and noticed the building was dedicated to an entire family.

We'll be seeing you on our side soon … a male ghost said. His English-accented baritone reminded her of Boris Karloff, making the hairs on the back of her neck stand on end.

No Starling closed her eyes. Leave me alone. I'm only visiting.

That's what we all say when we first step foot in this place, but people like you … you have no hope. Your spirit will easily be taken by those who reside here.

Starling pulled tightly against Jasper's side. "Let's hurry."

"Section E is just ahead. Are you okay?"

"Yeah," Starling replied, trying to summon the last bits of her waning courage. "The spirits here are restless."

Jasper's footfalls sped up and she raced to stay beside him.

A black wrought iron fence came into view, its bars tipped with spikes. On the gate was the name Gracie Watson.

"Epione didn't mention where we would find the books."

Jasper shook his head. "Do you think you can talk to Gracie? Maybe she can tell us something."

"I can try, but it doesn't always work," Starling said, taking hold of the metal growing cool in the evening hours. Inside the fence on the ground was a memorial telling the story of how Gracie had passed away from pneumonia at the age of six. Her sadness grew; the spirits of children were the most wrenching when they came to Starling and asked for help.

By her feet was a marker with the girl's last name, Watson. Small pebbles had been placed at the top and a dead leaf littered the corner. Reaching down, Starling brushed the leaf away. She rested her hand on the stone and shut her eyes.

Gracie? She concentrated, hoping to hear a child's voice, but no one answered. Gracie, are you here?

Nothing.

Gracie, my goddess, Epione, sent me here for a collection of books. She said you could help me. Are you here?

No answer.

"Is it working?" Jasper asked.

Starling shook her head.

"Remember what the cabby said about people putting gifts and money in her hand? It's worth a shot."

"How are we going to get through the gates to reach her?"

"Don't worry," he said with a wicked smile, "I got this." He pulled out his wallet and grabbed a wire-type tool. After a few well-practiced motions, he picked the lock, and the gate squeaked opened.

"You must have done well in bodyguard school," Starling said, acutely that she was in the presence of a man who could, if necessary, be deadly.

"Oh, I learned that way before I trained to be a bodyguard."

There was so much she didn't know about him. Then again, did she want to know Jasper Gray? Undoubtedly, he would only hurt her again. And even if she did open her heart, it would only put him in danger. Her kind couldn't love.

"Hand me some coins. I'll go in," Starling said, trying to think about anything but how close they were to one another.

Jasper pulled the money out of his pocket and handed it over.

Sliding through the barely opened gate, Starling walked over to the statue and dropped the money into the little girl's hand.

Gracie? Please come to me. I need your help. Please.

A child's laughter filtered through the trees and down on her.

Sweetheart, are you here?

There was a tug on Starling's pants leg. Looking down, she couldn't see anything, but her skin was cold.

"Hi, Gracie. It's nice to meet you."

Hi… The little girl answered shyly. *Can you see me?*

Starling shook her head. "I'm sorry, I wish I could, but I'm not magic. I can only talk to you."

Did you come to play?

"Would you like to?" she asked.

It's been a long time since someone wanted to play.

"What do you like? Do you know 'Ring Around the Rosie?'" She couldn't miss the irony in singing a children's song about the dying with a dead girl.

I love that song. But we need someone else to fall with us. What about the man?

Starling turned to Jasper. "She wants you to help us sing the song. You up for it?"

He made his way into the little yard that surrounded the girl's grave, but his eyes scanned the square like he was searching for something. "Sure," he said, sounding apprehensive.

"It's okay, she won't hurt you." Starling turned back to the girl's statue. "You won't hurt my friend Jasper, will you?"

Nuh uh, ma'am. But there are others here who are bad. They do bad things. They hurt people.

Chills ran down Starling's spine. "Who are these others, Gracie?"

The bad ones.

Starling's hand turned cold as the ghost must have slipped her icy hand into hers.

Let's not talk about them; let's just dance.

Reaching over, Starling slipped her free hand into Jasper's. He glanced down at his other hand. "My fingers are cold. Does that mean she's touching me?"

Starling nodded. "It's a strange feeling, isn't it?"

Jasper's face was pale as he nodded.

"You okay with this?"

"I'm fine," he said, but the color didn't return to his face.

Ring around the rosies, Gracie sang.

Starling nudged Jasper as she picked up the song. "Pockets full of posies. Ashes. Ashes. We all fall down." Starling fell to the ground, her head landing in Jasper's lap.

"Sorry." She sat up and away from Jasper's touch.

"It's okay," he replied.

The girl's laughter filled the silence. *That was fun. Let's do it again!*

"Gracie, I am looking for a collection of books. Can you help me?"

The girl's laughter stopped. *What books?*

"They're called the *Libros Umbrarum.* Have you heard of them?"

Yes.

"Do you know where I can find them?"

The girl didn't answer.

"I need them. The spirits have told me that they will help me gain control over the voices I hear. Please?"

Starling tried to quell her nerves. Gracie was only a little girl—there was no guarantee that she could, or would, help. If she didn't, they would be left at square one—no answers and the fear of attack. "Gracie, did you hear me?"

They're with the bad people. I don't want to go there.

"You don't have to go anywhere. You can stay right here and keep singing while we go, but you need to tell me where the books are, sweetheart."

Jasper gave her a questioning look, but she waved him off. "Where are the books, honey?"

The cold returned in Starling's hand followed by a light squeeze.

"Are you going to show me?"

There was a tug on her arm and Starling moved in the direction the little girl urged, summoning her courage for the sake of the child. Jasper followed as they made their way down the path and toward an archangel. The angel looked down on the grass, its wings spread slightly open, as if any moment it would take flight to the heavens. Her hands were open, palms up, ready to receive. At the base of the angel, the grave marker read: Avi Mortem, December 12, 1896.

"Jasper, have you ever heard of this Avi?" Starling whispered.

He shook his head.

The tugging stopped as they came within a step of the angel.

Put your hand in hers. Gracie squeezed Starling's fingers.

Reaching up, Starling slipped her hand into the angel's.

"Now what?" Starling asked.

You have to say the special words. You have to say: Avi Mortem, find comfort in the arms of the wicked and solace where no other dares. Mortem. Genus. Honor.

Starling repeated the chant and as the last word rolled from her tongue, the angel's stony fingers trembled. In what seemed like slow motion, the marble wings opened, exposing a long set of stairs leading below ground.

She stepped to the top of the stairs and looked down. A cold breeze blew upward from the cavernous black abyss at her feet. She took a step down.

"No." Jasper stopped her. "You can't do this. You have no idea what you are going to find down there."

"What choice do I have, Jasper?" She could have been hurtling toward her death, but if she didn't act, she would go crazy. "I can't quit now when I'm so close."

"Do you really think you can trust Gracie? How do you know she isn't trying to lure you into a trap?" Jasper looked around like he was waiting for the ghostly child to kick him in the shins. "You said the spirits have been threatening you. Not everyone is good."

She reached over and took Jasper's hand. "And regardless of what you may think, not everyone is bad. Sometimes you just have to have faith that everything will turn out all right."

Chapter Nine

The wind kicked up, sending a damp chill through the graveyard. Yet the chill on his skin was nothing compared to the chill in his soul. No matter how hard he tried, he couldn't find Starling's spirit of hope. Everything wouldn't turn out *all right*. It never did. No matter how hard you tried to avoid trouble or keep people safe, bad things always seemed to have a way of happening—but not this time.

"You can't go down there, Starling. You need to stay here, where it's safe."

She stared at him like he had lost his mind. "You can't tell me what to do, Jasper."

"I'm not telling you anything," he said, looking down at the way her hand fit perfectly into his palm. "I want to keep you from getting hurt, that's all. I'll go down there. You just yell whatever Gracie tells you. That way at least I know you won't be put into any more danger. Please, can you do that for me?"

Starling stepped back from the stairs, a look of shock on her face. "I'm only staying up here because you asked like you did. But if I call and you don't answer, or something happens, I'm coming down there. And there's nothing you can do to stop me. Agreed?"

He let go of her hand. "Got it, but you stay safe, too, okay?"

"I'm surrounded by my people," Starling said waving at the rows of the dead. "And Gracie's got my back. Nothing to worry about. Don't trip going down the stairs." She smiled tentatively, but her gaze moved steadily around their surroundings, like she was taking over his job as bodyguard.

He descended the stairs, his footsteps echoing. "Gracie saying anything?"

"Not yet," she yelled down.

The narrow stairwell smelled of wet decay, like rotting leaves after a fall storm. Was it the earth around him, or the bodies that lay entombed in that ground creating the smell? The thought made goose pimples rise on his arms. It wasn't death that scared him; no, he'd been around the dying enough to become accustomed to the rainbow bridge. It was something more, something he couldn't quite put his finger on. Maybe it was the permanence or the fear of what came after. Regardless, every cell of his body screamed for him to get out of this cellar in the cemetery.

"Where are the books?" Jasper yelled up toward Starling as he continued downward and deeper in the all-consuming darkness.

Starling mumbled something he couldn't quite hear. "Gracie says you need to look in the farthest room. She isn't sure exactly where."

Shit.

"Got it." Jasper took his cell phone out of his pocket and clicked on the light. He reached the bottom and the stairwell opened into a rectangular room that reminded him of the mausoleums they had passed in the cemetery. In the corner of the room was a small basin next to a concrete slab. In front of him, two chairs were set up against the wall, and between them was a wooden door about five feet tall, but the room was otherwise empty.

For the first time since he'd flown into Savannah, he wished he had brought his gun. Crossing the room was like walking naked through a high school, waiting for the cheerleading squad to spot his pale ass.

"You okay up there?" he called, trying to ignore his growing trepidation.

"Yep," Starling answered in a clipped voice.

He twisted the door handle. The door opened with a creak he'd only heard in horror movies. Shining the light in front of him, this room looked as empty as the first, and he stepped through the door.

It squeaked shut behind him.

Jasper spun around, reaching down over the side of his waist for a gun that wasn't there. "What the fuck?" He shined the light around the room, but the little cell phone light failed to brighten much. "Who's here?"

There was no answer.

Damn spirits.

"Starling, can you tell *your people* to lay off?" he yelled.

There was no answer from above. He tried to tell himself that the door must have muffled his sound, but his heart pounded.

It was too much. He wanted to help her, but he shouldn't have come down here—at least not without an exorcist. He reached for the door handle.

He twisted the brass handle, but as it turned, the knob fell off into his hand. "Son of a bitch …"

"Starling?" He yelled at the top of his lungs, letting the brass knob drop to the ground with a metallic thump. "I need help! The door broke!" He tried to ignore his racing heart and the fact that he was stuck underneath a haunted graveyard in a room no one besides he, Starling, and a ghost knew existed.

"Starling!"

No answer.

He pressed his ear against the cold door to listen for footsteps, but there was nothing. Not a sound.

Lowering his cell phone, he scrolled through his contacts, clicked on Starling's name, and pressed send. The phone flashed and an error message popped up reading: No Service. As soon as he got out of this hole in the ground, he would be having words with his cell phone company. Then again, what would he tell them— that he'd been stuck in a grave and didn't have service? Maybe not.

Taking a deep breath, he tried to center himself. He pushed on the door, but it didn't move. Using the little nub where the handle had been, he tried to get a hold and pull, but the door didn't budge.

"Starling!" But his voice only echoed through the room, and all he could hear was the fear in his voice.

Now wasn't the time to freak out. His training had prepared him for this … this … entrapment.

Adrenaline poured into his system. Taking ten steps back, he ran forward and launched his shoulder into the stubborn door. Pain coursed through him as he reeled back from the hit.

"Don't tell me the fucking door is haunted," he said aloud.

It's not, a man answered.

"What the fuck?" Jasper turned and pressed his back against the wall. "Who's here?"

Silence.

"Who is here? Answer me now or I'll start shooting," he warned, reaching down to his side, trying to fake carrying a gun.

Come now, the man said, *we both know you do not possess a sidearm.*

Fuck.

He aimed his light in the direction of the voice but met only more darkness.

"What do you want?" he asked the mysterious voice.

I wish to receive answers…

"Come into the light," Jasper ordered, as he tried to steady the phone's light in front of him. "I want to know who I'm talking to."

Are you sure that is what you want? Most don't wish to see me or my kind.

What was that supposed to mean? "Who are you?"

I'm the thing that children fear in the night. I'm the shadow that seems to change form in front of your eyes, the thing at the edge of your vision. I'm the feeling in your gut when you think you are being watched.

"Don't play games with me."

Oh, I'm going to do much more than play games with you. The man's voice became a whisper.

A shiver ran down Jasper's spine. "Where the fuck are you?"

He frantically patted at his waist and then his pockets, searching for anything he could use as a weapon. The only thing he had besides his wallet was the phone in his hand. If the man in the room really was a ghost, there was little he could do to protect himself physically, with or without a weapon. Yet, if the man was a real, tangible being, he was willing to do anything to keep himself safe so he could get back up to Starling.

You can't see me? I'm right here …

Something ruffled Jasper's hair on the side of his head. He jerked the light around, but there was nothing only more darkness. "Real funny. Let me out of here."

Not before I take what I need.

"What do you need?" Jasper gripped his phone tighter, trying in vain to stop the light from shaking in his hand.

I need your body, the man whispered into his ear.

An icy energy seeped into his ear, seeped down his neck. He tried to move, but the cold energy moved deeper, taking over his limbs.

"Stop. Don't. Just tell me what you want! I have to protect Starling. You can't do this!"

I can do whatever I please. You must do my bidding. I need to find my revenge. Is that not why you are here? To be my slave? They told me you were coming.

The cold moved up his face. "They?" he forced the word from his numb lips.

Your friends. The vultures. The man laughed. *By the way, they send their warmest regards. They are looking forward to receiving the ugly duckling, Starling.*

•••

"Jasper?" There was no answer. Her footsteps echoed as she raced down the marble stairwell. The swamp-scented darkness swallowed her, forcing her to stop and pull her phone from her purse. "Jasper, where are you?"

She flicked on the flashlight. Lifting the light, she peered beyond its glow. Standing in the light, shielding his eyes, was Jasper.

"Why are you here?" he asked, his voice deep and raspy.

"I told you I would come down at the first sign of trouble. You agreed."

He eyed her like he was forming some kind of plan. "Fine," Jasper answered, but his voice remained far from his baritone.

"Are you okay, Jasper?"

Jasper walked by her, bumping her as he made his way past and up the stairs.

"Jasper?" She turned and jogged up the stairs after him. "What's going on? What was down there?"

He didn't slow down or bother to answer.

"What in the hell?" She grabbed him by the arm, trying to get him to stop.

Jasper turned. His lips were curled up, like a feral dog ready to bite. "Do not touch me again, Jezebel."

She let go of his arm and drew back from his blow. "What's wrong with you?"

"Nothing more than I do not have time for you. Go find yourself another … lover."

Jasper had never called her his lover. Something wasn't right. "Did you find the books?"

He frowned at her. "I care nothing of books. Or you. So be gone."

He stepped out of the open wings of the angel and into the night. This person walking away from her looked like Jasper, but he couldn't possibly be the same man who had put himself at risk by going underground.

I'm sorry, Gracie said. *I didn't know…*

"You didn't know what, Gracie?"

Starling felt the little girl throw her arms in a hug around her waist. *I didn't know he would be taken.*

She looked down, but there was nothing to see that indicated the ghostly child held her aside from feeling her touch. "Is he," Starling motioned toward the man with her chin, "Jasper, or is this some other magical being?"

It's Jasper, but Edward has taken over his body.

Who's Edward?

The bad one.

She tried not to lose her patience with the child. It wasn't Gracie's fault that she didn't understand.

"Sweetheart, why would Edward want to take over Jasper?"

I dunno. He always talks about his wife and what a powerful woman she was. I don't like him. He's always yelling.

The gravel crunched as Jasper made his way through the cemetery, making a beeline for the nearest street.

"Jasper, stop!" Starling yelled after.

The man kept walking.

"Edward, stop! I can help you if you let me."

The man turned on his heel. "How do you know my name?"

"Wait for me!" she hollered across the cemetery.

She stepped out of the ghostly girl's arms. "You stay here. Stay safe, Gracie."

I'll miss you, Starling.

The girl's words pulled at her heart's strings. "I'll be back, honey. Don't worry; we'll play."

Gracie didn't answer, but Starling had to go. "I'll be back. Really."

She jogged across the cemetery, careful to step around the rectangular graves.

Jasper stood waiting. "How do you know my name?"

"Is Jasper still in there?" She stared into Jasper's hazel eyes. Deep in the blue ring at their centers, she saw a flicker of light.

"Is that his name, this man?" He looked down at his body. "Hmm, fitting."

"Jasper, if you can hear me, I've got this. I got your back."

The man put his hands akimbo. The movement was so unlike Jasper that it caught Starling off guard. "What is that supposed to mean, Jezebel?"

"I'm not a hooker. The name's Starling."

"Starling. Like the bird?"

"Yes, like the bird. Now, why did you take over my friend's body?"

"I do as I please, and I hardly believe that I must answer to you, little bird."

Anger seeped through her. "In case you've been living in that cave for the last 100 years and missed the memo, women aren't treated like property any more. We have a voice and aren't afraid to use it. So you can either start being polite, or I personally guarantee that I'll find a way to get your soul sent straight to hell."

"Little spitfire I see." The man laughed. "Well, while I revel in the fact that you feel so free to speak your mind, I see no reason to seek your approval any more than I would seek approval from a mangy dog."

"You did not just say that ..." Starling recoiled, her cheeks burning.

She had been threatened, scolded, told what to do, and put down by spirits before, but she'd never been angrier. If it weren't Jasper's almost perfect body that would take the assault, she would pummel the man. Yet the man who stood in front of her was no longer Jasper—at least for now.

The man readjusted the shirt, flattening it over his stomach. "Now if you will excuse me, it's been almost 100 years since I've been able to leave this place, and I've things to attend to."

"What do you possibly have to do after 100 years?"

"I have a being to kill. There's nothing sweeter than the taste of revenge. Then I will need to die a proper death. This time I'm not going to be stuck in the torments of the spiritual realm. Heaven waits."

"Let me get this straight. You came back to kill someone and then you *believe* you are going to get into heaven?" Starling scoffed. "I admit it's been a while since I thumbed through a bible, but I'm pretty sure that killing a human isn't going to get the Big Guy to open the pearly gates."

"You know nothing. Murder is only murder if it's committed against a human. In this instance, it will be like slaughtering a pig. Except this pig's death shall be nothing less than glorious. In fact, I wouldn't be surprised if the Lord gives me some type of award for such an act of valor." The man turned away and made his way to the busy Bonaventure Way road.

"You do realize it's not the 1800s anymore. You won't be able to find your way around the city."

"I beg to disagree," Edward replied, without bothering to look back. "I will find some kind soul willing to help me find my destination."

"I think you're vile, and I'm about the kindest soul you are going to find."

"I find that hard to believe, wench."

"Well, you are welcome to go." She gave him a wicked smile. "Just make sure you don't get hit by a car when you try to cross the highway. I don't care about you, but I want Jasper back."

He stopped. Edward turned. "Fine. If you are so adamant about being included, you can act as my servant."

"Do I need to remind you that I will send you to hell? I'm no one's servant."

"Beg pardon," Edward said with an over-the-top bow. "My lady, thou shalt be treated as the little bird thee are."

Thank God culture had changed. If men today acted like this overstuffed spirit, she would be in prison for manslaughter.

"Try it again. I want a real apology."

Edward kneeled down in front of her and took her hand in his. "My lady Starling, forgive my rudeness." He kissed the back of her hand. Jasper's warm lips made her heart stutter and she pulled her hand from his fingers.

If Edward was desperate enough for her help to apologize, then he must be hellbent on finding justice, and desperation could drive a person to extremes.

She had only two options: try to use her almost non-existent powers as a medium to control the spirit and get him to leave Jasper's body, or help the man to get his revenge. Neither would be easy. If she relied on her powers, there was no guarantee that they would work, and if she somehow managed to banish the ghost from Jasper, there was no telling what would happen. She couldn't imagine a life without Jasper—even if he was a pain in the ass.

The quicker she helped Edward, the quicker he would release his grip on Jasper, and they could get back to work and out of this hellhole.

Starling walked in the direction of the parked taxi. "Tell me about him."

"First of all, it's not a *him*. Her name is Bethany Fortenberry."

"What did she do that made you hold a grudge for this many years?"

"She cursed my family. Her poisonous tongue cost the lives of my wife and child. She must be made to pay for the pain she caused not only me, but my family."

"There is no bringing back the dead."

"No, but it will bring me peace. Once I find my justice, I can happily pass to the other side."

"So you will leave Jasper's body?"

Edward glanced at her, a look of annoyance on his face. "I may, but you must agree to help me."

Chapter Ten

The Goddess Shop's windows were dark and the open light had been turned off for the night, but Starling couldn't wait. Jasper needed her.

"Where are you taking me?" Edward asked, getting out of the taxi and closing the door.

"You said you needed to kill Bethany. Well, Jamie is the woman to go to. She'll have everything we need."

"I have hands and willpower, I need nothing more," he retorted.

"Yeah, let's just imagine how *that* would play out. Ding-dong. Who is it? Edward. I'm here to kill you." Starling snorted. "I bet she'll let you in, no problem."

"You think I'm a novice? That I haven't spent years thinking about how I would go about killing her? You are worse than a mangy dog—at least they have the ability to think ahead."

Edward reminded her of Jasper chastising her for her failure to plan at the airport. She leaned forward so their noses almost touched and peered into Jasper's blue-rimmed eyes. Had some of Jasper's thoughts leaked through to the man's words? Was he in there somewhere?

"What are you doing?" The spirit stepped back, affronted by her closeness.

"Just looking for something." She relaxed, satisfied that she had seen nothing more than her own reflection in Edward's eyes. She would find nothing there—no, she would have to search deeper to find the man she was looking for.

"What is this place?" he asked, his lip pulled up into a sneer as he looked up at the purple awning that blocked the moon from shining on their heads.

"It's a store." She knocked on the door. The sound was hollow and empty as it reverberated through the quiet store and back to them.

The window display was backlit, showing an array of antique books and pentagrams, but no other lights were on.

"Is this a shop of witchcraft?" Edward huffed. "Your people allow such devils to roam free and proudly display their paganism?"

"They're not devils, they're normal … well normal-ish. And you can thank the freedom of religion provision in the first amendment. Everyone is free to follow their religious preference. No more Salem witch hunts."

"I'm familiar with the First Amendment, however I never thought it would be taken to such a liberal extent."

"Isn't America wonderful?" Starling smiled. "No more corsets, women can vote, and we are allowed to follow our hearts. Freedom at its finest."

"Quite the feminist."

"Nope, just a modern American woman." Starling knocked again.

A stray cat ran across the road, yowling at some unknown assailant while a woman yelled somewhere in the distance.

"Hmm, what a fine place this world has become. For the first time since my demise, I admit that I'm happy to be dead."

"Well, don't worry. If I have my way, you'll be right back in your grave where you belong."

The door's blinds moved back and Jamie's head poked into view. The witch smiled as she recognized Starling. Unclicking the locks, she opened the door. "Starling! So glad to see you. I'm sorry I didn't know you were comin' or I woulda fixed some tea."

A bird screeched from somewhere in the back.

"Thank you for answering the door. I wasn't sure you lived here." She made her way into the darkened shop. It had been homey in the daytime, but being here at night, surrounded by the occult made her nervous, like she had entered the most sacred of holy places.

"No problem, I'm glad you came. I've got some things I wanted to ask you about your gift. Jasper," she added with an acknowledging nod.

"Vile witch," Edward answered, his greeting as dry and flat as the soul.

"What?" Jamie closed the door behind him.

"Don't mind him. He's possessed by a ghost named Edward who's hellbent on finding revenge. Let's just say we didn't find what we were looking for at the Bonaventure Cemetery."

"One seldom does." Jamie laughed. "If you had told me you were going there, I could have made you a protection spell or taught you a chant to help." Jamie glanced over at her. "Maybe I could have helped Jasper."

"Speaking of that … " Starling pulled the amethyst Jamie had given her from her pocket. "The stone didn't keep the spirits from talking to me. I think you can have it back."

The purple crystal looked almost black in the darkness of the room.

"You didn't become possessed, did you?" Jamie took Starling's hand in her warm touch. "The stone did just as it was intended." She curled Starling's fingers around the crystal and glanced over at Edward who, just like Jasper, kept his back pressed against the door.

"I don't think it works. Here," Starling repeated, handing Jamie the stone.

She tried not to notice Jamie's look of disapproval as she dropped the stone back into its container. "No matter how powerful the stone, it would never help a non-believer."

"Right now," Starling whispered, "I'm more worried about saving Jasper. But Edward thinks I'm here to help him find a woman."

"Understood." Jamie's gaze moved to Edward.

"What did you just say?" Edward asked.

"Nothing," Jamie said in a motherly voice. "She was tellin' me 'bout you bein' in some sort of trouble. I'm fixin' to help."

"Witch, I find it hard to comprehend that you should be able to help me. I'm a God-fearing Christian man, not some pagan."

Jamie's soft smile turned hard. "I help many who believe themselves to be God-fearing Christians. Everyone needs a little assistance from the other side once in a while. First, you tell me what you need, and then I'll see if I can help you. If not, no harm done, right?"

He gave her a sideways glance. "I'm looking for a woman. You may have heard of her, that is, if she's still residing in the city. Her name is Bethany Fortenberry."

Jamie's eyes widened and her mouth opened, exposing her metal-filled teeth. She turned to Starling. "Lord a'mighty, how did you get yourself into this mess?"

"What can I say? I'm just lucky," she said, trying to make light of the utter look of horror on the woman's face. "Do you know where we can find her?"

"Come with me," Jamie answered, motioning toward the purple curtain covering the door to the back of the shop. "You," she said to Edward, "stay here. You understand?"

Edward glanced around the shop but after a moment, he nodded.

Their footsteps echoed on the wood floor as Jamie ushered her to the back and closed the curtain far enough to block them from Edward's sight.

"Do you know who Bethany Fortenberry is?" Jamie hissed.

"She's not Mother Teresa, I'm guessing?"

"Ms. Bethany is the Voodoo Queen."

Starling laughed as she envisioned a woman wearing a scarf wrapped around her head, holding a snake, and chanting in tongues like some character out of a cheap horror movie. "You have got to be kidding. There's no such thing as voodoo."

"Voodoo isn't just for the tourists, Ms. Starling. What Ms. Bethany does is very real and very dangerous. You don't want to go messin' with her."

"Go to hell …" A shrill voice sounded from the shadows in the corner of the back of the room. "Go to hell," it repeated.

"Excuse me?" Starling peered into the shadows but saw only darkness.

"Don't worry about that, Ms. Starling. It's only my parrot. He thinks he's funny."

"You have a parrot who cusses?"

"Unfortunately. That little bugger has been doing that ever since … " Jamie trailed off. "Never mind about the parrot. He's nothing but a bother."

Something about the way she trailed off sparked Starling's curiosity, but she had a long list of things she needed to worry about before she could be concerned with a swearing parrot. "Can you help me get rid of Edward? I need Jasper to help me get the books I came after, and he's no good to me if he's being led by a ghost."

"We can try to do an exorcism, but I have a feeling it's going to be tricky to get him to agree to it," Jamie said with a sigh. "I can't say I've been through something like this before. I'm afraid I'm not going to be a lotta use to you."

"There has to be something you can do, some spell or something."

"There's nothing I can think of that won't hurt your friend Jasper in the process of trying to rid him of the spirit. You don't wanna risk hurting him, do you?" Jamie gave her a questioning look, as if she was trying to gauge exactly how much Jasper meant to her.

"No," she said, shaking her head. "We can't put him at risk. We'll just have to help Edward with his hunt for the Voodoo Queen."

"Your Jasper's going to be in just as much danger, if not more, if you go after her. She has one nasty temper and an even nastier bag of tricks."

"So what do you think I should do if I can't help him, and you can't help me?"

Jamie paused for a moment, thinking. "You know how a spirit leaves a body?"

"Other than exorcism, I have no idea."

"Yes, an exorcism is one, but the easiest way to get a spirit to leave a body is for them to choose to."

There was a crash and the sound of shattering glass from the front room.

"Edward, what are you doing?" Starling called as she rushed out of the darkened backroom and into the store's main area.

He stood in the center of a pool of shattered glass. He held one of the wands, which he sat back down on a shelf when he noticed her. "I really don't think having so many breakable things in such a small area is advisable. I was doing you a service by showing you what could have happened to one of your customers due to your lack of organizational skills."

"You've gotta be kidding me," Jamie said. "You really think you can blame this on my housekeeping skills when you were acting dumber than a bag of boiled peanuts in my shop? You're just lucky that I can't throw you out."

"I'd be happy to leave your establishment. It's the devil's playground."

"Like you have any room to judge me. You are the one who is trying to mess with Bethany," Jamie scoffed. "At least I know who to treat with some level of respect. I'm not like you, going around poking at wild cats."

"I only give respect to those whom I deem worthy. I'm not a lapdog, nor am I subservient to anyone—witch or not."

"You are lucky you're dead. If you weren't, I would give my left foot to help Bethany take you down."

"Go to hell!" the parrot screeched.

"I never ... " Edward flushed with rage.

"Let's go, Edward, before I help Jamie turn you into a frog." Starling could just imagine him hopping around on the broken glass on the floor. One thing was certain—as a frog, he would have been easier to handle.

"It would be my pleasure." The glass crunched under him as he made his way to the door. "May we never meet again." He slammed the door.

"I'm sorry about that, Starling," Jamie said, running the back of her hand over her forehead. "I don't deal well with people whose fear and misunderstanding turns to hatred and bullying. I hope you can get rid of that devil before something really bad happens."

"Me too, Jamie, me too." Starling glanced out the door. Edward stood with his arms crossed over his chest and he talked to himself. "And tell your parrot thank you," she said. "I've wanted to tell this spirit to go to hell since the moment I met him."

Jamie walked to the corner and grabbed a broom. "You ain't the only one. But I'm guessin' if you meet up with that Bethany, he may get his chance."

"About Bethany … do you know where I can find her?"

The broom swished over the hardwood, collecting the glass into a pile. "That's easy. She's a few blocks down on the left and she lives above her shop."

"Thank you, Jamie. For everything."

"You just stay safe, Starling. And I didn't think I would say this, but I hope you get your Jasper back soon."

...

"You lied to me," Edward growled. "You told me that shop would have what I need to take down Bethany. Your deceit will cost you."

There was nothing more he could take from her. As it was, she had nothing—no hope, her life was in danger, and Jasper was possessed. The only thing Edward could do to make things worse was to hurt Jasper, and she would never let that happen—she couldn't.

"I didn't deceive you." She glanced behind her toward the shop to make sure Jamie wasn't listening. "I got what we needed."

"A verbal accosting is hardly what I needed."

The cabby pointed to his vehicle and mouthed something—probably the amount she was running up on the meter. There went her last bit of cash. She raised her finger, letting him know they would be a minute.

"Just because we didn't buy anything doesn't mean I didn't get help." Her footsteps echoed through the barren city street. The street lamps flickered to life, casting long skeletal shadows on the sidewalk. Instinctively, she stepped closer to Jasper, but moved a step away as she remembered who he had become. "I know where we can find Bethany."

Even in the dim light, Edward's eyes brightened. "That's brilliant."

"If I take you there, you promise to leave Jasper unhurt?"

"I will do my best to keep your friend intact." He smiled, but just like his words, it lacked sincerity.

Her stomach churned. "Is there any way, any way at all that I can keep you from going after her? I will kill her myself if you would just promise to leave Jasper."

"I have waited decades for the chance to see this foul wench face to face. There's nothing you could give me to sway me from my course, that is, unless you have her head on a platter."

"I will give it to you if that is what you want." Starling stopped. "I have a gift of talking to the dead. Maybe there's a way I can get them to help us. If she's as bad as you say, there have to be others she has wronged."

"You make it sound simple, but you don't know spirits, do you?"

"I know they can be enormous pains in the ass, present company included."

He waved her off. "Spirits aren't pets. They can't be called by an inexperienced medium. Only the truly powerful can summon a spirit, not to mention a large group of them."

She leaned in. "I didn't come to Savannah for a vacation. I came down here to grow my skills. And, I know there are books somewhere here that will give me the power to control and do as I wish with spirits. All I have to do is find the books—then we will have your army."

That was if the Catharterians didn't get to her first.

"Where are these books?" There was a strange glint of malice in his eye.

"They were supposed to be in your grave. That's why Jasper went down there. Did you see any books in your time in the mausoleum?"

Edward tapped his finger against his chin. "Maybe I did, hard to say. My many visitors always had an assortment of things."

"What kind of visitors did you get?"

"As I'm sure you are aware, vultures are attracted to death."

"You're saying the Catharterians were there?"

"They more than visited. It's their headquarters."

"Their headquarters?" she asked, stunned by Edward's admission.

Edward answered with a sly smile.

Jasper would have killed for the information and now, when it mattered most, he couldn't act—at least not on his own accord—but she could take control. She could help Jasper's investigation while she worked to set his body free of the entrapment of Edward's soul.

"If it's their headquarters, then the books must be there," Starling said, her excitement spilling into her voice, but under her thin layer of giddiness was a reservoir of apprehension.

"Don't get ahead of yourself. Let's first find Bethany."

"I'll have to try to call the ghosts for help."

"No, Starling. We don't need an army."

"Okay. We don't need an army, but we need a real plan instead of this Wild West thing you have going on. You aren't going to go in without a weapon and take down the Savannah Voodoo Queen—no matter how badly you want to."

"What makes you think I don't have a weapon?"

"Did you steal something from Jamie? If you did, you're going back in there and paying." As the words spilled from her lips, she realized how much she sounded like her mother. An unexpected loneliness filled her at the thought.

"I'm not a child. I don't steal."

Her empty laugh drew waves in her lake of loneliness. "You *stole* my friend."

He waved her off. "Hardly the same thing."

"Yes, stealing a human body is far worse."

"If everything goes as it should, your friend will remain uninjured and everything will be taken care of. All you have to do is tell me where Bethany is."

"I'll tell you only if you tell me exactly what you are planning. You say you have weapons, but I don't see anything. You talk about a plan, but so far you seem lost. What's going on?"

"What if I told you I have seen one of your books? That your dear friends, the Catharterians, have been using me to protect their little secrets?"

Her breath caught in her throat. He had to be kidding. "Don't lie to me."

"I speak the truth."

Was it possible this awful being held the answers she had been looking for? "What are the books called?"

"The *Libros Umbrarum*." Edward smiled, his white teeth sparkling in the dim lamplight. "The book I saw was made of perfect white vellum, so soft that it is like a baby's skin. Each page was hand painted with gold-infused oils. The book was truly a work of art."

"What do they say about dealing with spirits?"

His smile widened. "I bet you would love to know. Perhaps, after Bethany's death, I can share the secrets I've learned."

"I don't want your secrets. I want answers."

Catching her off guard, Edward grabbed her around the waist and pulled her into his lips. His kiss was unrushed, unyielding, and for a second too long, she relished the way he took her just as she had imagined Jasper doing for so long. She opened her eyes and looked up as his lips roamed hers. Looking into his eyes, she saw only Edward looking back at her. Disgusted not at the kiss, but at the spirit behind it, she pushed him away.

Edward laughed as he dabbed at the wetness left by her kiss. "Jasper sends his best."

"Jasper? He's … in there?" she stammered as she stared for some sign of her friend, but found nothing.

"I did not wish to kiss some lost girl," Edward retorted. "If you ask me, Jasper is lowering himself to be with you."

"We're not together."

Edward's eyebrow rose. "If that's true, then he certainly needs to restrain his inappropriate thoughts toward you."

Inappropriate thoughts? Jasper did care for her more than just as a friend. But if that were true, why had he waited so long to make himself known? Was it all a ploy to use her to get rid of Edward? No. If he was inside his body, he had to see that she was already doing everything in her power. That meant his kiss had to be real—or not—and the only way she could know for sure was to have him back. "So you can hear his thoughts?"

"If you continue with me, Starling, you will get the answers you seek."

Chapter Eleven

It was a strange thing, but Starling missed Jasper even though he stood right next to her. His hair was the same disheveled mess, his chin carried the same dimple, but the look in his eyes would have never belonged to him. And, maybe that was what she missed the most. She'd never really noticed the way he looked at her, but now that Edward had taken his place, all she could remember was the way his gaze had felt on her skin—like a warm hand, it would move over her body, enjoying the subtle curves of her hips, leaving behind a trail of wanting.

"Bethany's shop is a few blocks down. She's probably not open now—it's after ten o'clock—but we can get the cabby to drive us by on the way back to the hotel and we can check."

"I do not care if she is open or not. I'm not going to her for business."

"Got it." She walked to the cab, opened the door, and slid into the backseat. "You coming?"

"Don't help him, Starling. He will never make good on his promise," Jasper said, his voice taking the place of Edward's.

"Jasper? Are you there? Is Edward gone?" She jumped out of the cab. The familiar warmth had returned to his desert-colored eyes.

Jasper stared at her like he wanted to move, but his body wouldn't obey him. "I am gaining. He's strong, but maybe I can break through. But this thing with the voodoo lady, he's not telling you the truth. You can't help him."

"If I don't help him, he's going to hurt you."

Jasper staggered toward her, wrapping his arms around her. "I don't matter. You are more important than a hundred of me." He leaned down and his lips met hers; this time his kiss was tender, deeper, and richer than the first. Yet, it quickly broke. He staggered backward and his face hardened.

"That won't happen again. Your friend will not break through my barrier." Edward's cold voice took the place of Jasper's subtle warmth. Edward made his way to the cab and climbed inside, but all she could think of were the remnants of Jasper's kiss.

There was no question about it—Jasper cared. Unfortunately, he was wrong about his worth. She could never let a monstrous spirit like Edward hurt the only man she'd ever been interested in. If Jasper truly knew her, he would have understood that she had learned her lesson about letting others control her fate—that mistake had already cost her mother's life. She couldn't lose anyone else she cared for, not when she could do something to stop the tragedy.

"Let's go. We have a woman to kill."

"Don't you care about what your Jasper said?" Edward asked.

"I do, but I happen to think that you are right in your anger toward Bethany. She killed your family. Anyone who can hurt an innocent woman and child deserves to be struck down."

"I'm glad you finally are beginning to see things my way. It will make this much easier than I had anticipated."

She got into the cab. "Take us to the voodoo shop, please."

The cabby glanced back at her in his rearview mirror. "Everything okay, miss?"

She looked away from his prying eyes. "Fine."

He put the car into gear and they made their way down the empty street. On the left was a blackened shop, with a wooden sign hung above the door that read: The Goat's Head. The shop's windows were painted with odd symbols and the open light had been turned off. "Let's go," she said as she opened the door and stepped out of the taxi. "You wanted your chance. Here it is. But remember, you owe me the books and my friend. If you go against me, I will find a way to send your spirit to the depths of hell even if I have to sell my soul to Zeus. I will make sure you never reach your family in the afterlife."

Edward cringed. "Regardless of what your Jasper thinks, I will come through. My word is my honor. Honor is the only thing I have besides my eternal soul. I take my vow in earnest."

"I hope so." She shifted uncomfortably at the thought of having to go to the nymphs' enemy—Zeus.

She walked up the steps to the door and knocked on the glass.

"Ain't nobody here. Get gone!" a woman answered.

"We need your help," Starling called back. "My friend thinks he's possessed by a demon." She cringed as she realized how her lie so closely resembled the truth. "We don't know where else to turn."

They were answered with silence.

Edward knocked on the door again. "Please ... I need help. Money isn't an issue."

The door opened a crack. A woman peered out through the tiny space. "I charge double after hours. Triple if you're a pain in the ass." She opened the door a tiny bit more. Catching sight of Edward, her face brightened. "What are you doing here, Edward?"

"It's been a while." He smiled. "Aren't you going to let us in?"

She opened the door and waved them in. "They're gonna be angry."

"I took initiative. They can't be angry. Not when I got what something they want." Edward grabbed Starling by the arm. She tried to resist, but he pushed her through the door in front of him.

"What they be wanting? What you mean? Who be this girl?"

"This is Starling. She's my prisoner."

Starling gasped. "What the hell are you talking about?" Starling pulled her arm out of Edward's hand as she looked around the dark shop, seeking another door for escape.

"You are such an imprudent woman," Edward said as he closed the door and clicked the lock into place.

Her heartbeat thundered in her ears. Jasper had been right; she never should have trusted Edward to do as he'd promised. How could she have been so stupid and fallen for the promises of a being who had nothing to lose?

"Did you lie about everything, Edward? Did your family even exist?"

The ebony-colored woman standing beside him laughed. "How long you gonna tell people that I be some evil murderer? Don't you get tired of the same ole lie? You gotta get some new material, Eddie."

"But it's fun and it always works. I always manage to find you."

"How did you go 'bout findin' me this time?" She flicked on one of the switches in a long line, lighting up the shop. The shelves were filled with different types of liquors, and strange marionette-style dolls hung from the ceiling by their slender necks.

"Your friend Jamie, the witch, pointed us in the direction of your new shop."

"Well, I'm mighty glad she did. You didn't give her no reason to suspect nothin', did ya? She's been itchin' to find something to use against me."

"Come now, Beth. We've been together too long for you to worry about such frivolous details." Edward pushed a stray hair out of Bethany's face and back up under her head wrap. "I'll always put you first, *mon cher*."

Starling ran her hand over her neck, as her body switched into autopilot in the face of danger. "What do you plan on doing with me?"

Bethany turned her neck, and as she moved, Starling noticed that her earrings were made of tiny bones and a sparkling blue stone. The Voodoo Queen frowned as she looked at Starling like she'd all but forgotten that she had been standing there. "That's a good question, Edward. What're ya plannin' on doin' with your little poppet?"

"You need to call them. I believe they will finally follow through on their promises to you and me once they have their hands on this girl."

"You be dreamin', Eddie." Bethany sat her hand lovingly on Edward's arm. "But I do have to admit I'm glad to be seeing ya. This body be one of the best so far."

Edward ran his hand down her cheek. "If we play our cards right, maybe this one I can keep."

"I hope so. I think we could have us a lot of fun." Bethany ran her finger over the buttons on Jasper's shirt and pulled back the hem just enough to show his bare skin. She raked her long, white-tipped fingernail over his washboard stomach, making Edward wince with enjoyment.

A strangled noise escaped Starling as she watched the woman defile Jasper's flesh. "Don't touch him."

Bethany glanced back at her. "You go mindin' your own business, girl. It's been a mighty long time since I've been with my Eddie. You're lucky I'm not lockin' you in the basement." She flashed Edward a wanton look.

"You have no business touching Jasper. He isn't just somebody you can use and throw away."

"Why? He yours?" Bethany asked with a spitting laugh, leaving her fingers on Jasper's pecs.

Starling stepped forward and batted the woman's hand away from Jasper. "I'm sick of you. I'm sick of this. I want him back."

Edward's laughter ricocheted through the macabre room. "See. She's a girl. I almost feel badly throwing her to the vultures. I have to admit, I'm a bit surprised they hadn't found her and brought her back to headquarters by now; she wasn't hard to manipulate. All I needed was to find her weak point—Jasper."

"Did you stop to think that maybe that's part of their plan, Eddie? What if they're using her for somethin'? What if they're angry at what you've gone and done?" Bethany huffed. "You shoulda at least told me before you took her."

"What was I going to do, Bethany? It was a spur-of-the-moment decision. And believe me, I thought long and hard about bringing her here—I didn't want to get you mixed up in any more business with the council. There was no other way around it. She wouldn't just tell me where to find you."

"You ever thought of looking in a phone book?" Bethany stepped out of his arms. "I made sure my address be everywhere so you could find me if you got the chance to come back."

"I don't see a lot of phone books lying around. Don't be angry with me, my pet. I tried to do the best I could. At least I finally found a body I could possess. Let's just be happy. This could be our chance to start again. Make a real go of life. We can travel. The world is our oyster."

"Only if the council fixes to let us live. They were fumin' after your last escape."

Edward glanced over at Starling like she was nothing more than a pile of garbage. "Maybe we don't have to turn her into the council. It will be a few days before they realize I've gone missing from the cemetery."

"Is that where they stuck you this time?" Bethany asked. "Which one? I went all round the city tryin' to find you."

"Bonaventure. They even let me have a nice little mausoleum. I think they are really starting to move past my last run for freedom."

"Well, now that forgiveness gonna be over." Bethany moved away from the door and pulled the shades down in her windows.

You can't let them take you. You have to get away. Asclepius's spectral voice echoed through Starling's mind. *They will kill you if you stay here.*

Starling stepped back, keeping her back against the wall so she could keep a close eye on her enemies. People want to kill me everywhere I go. What am I going to do? I can't leave Jasper in their hands.

If you don't act, they'll send you to the Catharterians or kill you themselves—either way, you'll never make it out of this city alive. You know what you need to do. You can do this. Your life depends on what happens in the next few moments.

Starling shuffled down the wall until she came to a counter.

"Where do you think you be goin'?" Bethany said, motioning for her to stop moving.

Starling stopped and put her hands behind her back. Her fingers brushed against something sharp. "I'm not going anywhere. I just wanted to give you guys your space."

"You're a little brat. You don't expect me think you ain't up to something, do you? Just a second ago you were throwin' a right fit about me touchin' your man and now you be actin' all quiet."

Starling took hold of the long, slightly sharp object. It felt metallic and cold, but she didn't risk looking behind her to see exactly what she'd found.

"What you got there in your hand?" Bethany took a step toward her.

Without thinking, Starling reacted, rushing at the Voodoo Queen with the mysterious object. She plunged the object into the space just above the woman's clavicle. Letting go, she saw the end of a silver candlestick.

"You bitch. What have you done!" Bethany screamed with anger and pain. "Edward, kill her. Kill the little bitch!"

Starling ran to the door and fumbled with the lock as Edward's fingers twisted around her throat. She pushed his right hand away. "No!" she screamed. Grabbing the nearest object, a bottle of sand, she twisted and threw it in his face. The bottle smashed against his nose, sending sand into his eyes.

She twisted the lock open while Edward cried out with pain. Starling nearly fell through the doorway and rushed down the street to where the cab was waiting.

"Go!" she yelled.

The cabby gave her a shocked look but hit the gas, screeching the tires as they escaped away in the night.

Chapter Twelve

Not only had she let herself down by allowing herself to be tricked by a terrible imposter, but she had also left Jasper behind and worse—hurt. She had wanted so badly to protect him from the terrible spirit and his mistress, but now there was no way she could go back. She had no one she could call on to help her—except Jamie. But if she called the witch, she would put her in danger, too.

Starling couldn't risk hurting anyone else. Her best bet was finding an answer to help Jasper on her own—which meant going back to the cemetery and finding the books. The books held the answers to control and manage spirits, which meant they may well hold the answer on how to remove Edward's spirit from Jasper's body. Jamie had said the books weren't her only answer, but maybe they could be the first answer in a long line of questions.

"Can you please take me back to the Bonaventure Cemetery?" she asked the driver. She glanced up at the meter. Thankfully, she still had a paid room, or she would have been resigned to living on the streets until she got Jasper back.

"You got it." The man turned toward the cemetery, driving slowly through the darkened streets. Everything was dark until they drove down Bay Street. The lights of the city were ablaze, making the mass of bar-goers glow red and green, gold and purple. Was that what most people her age were doing? Living life to the fullest, unencumbered by the death of their mother and loss of their only friend?

For a moment, jealousy splashed through her, but it was quickly replaced with gut-wrenching fear.

She had acted impulsively, but no matter how much she replayed the scene in her head, she couldn't think of another way to have gotten out of The Goat's Head alive and with Jasper at her side. And if she didn't make it, neither would Jasper.

The cab came to a stop in front of the sign for the cemetery. "You want me to wait here again?"

"Please." Hopefully she would be coming back. She handed the cabby most of the money that was left in her purse.

The damp night air hung on her like a wet shower curtain, chilling her to the core. She of all people shouldn't be afraid of entering a graveyard at night, but she couldn't stop the anxiety that built up inside her as she made her way past row after row of grave markers.

What are you doing back? Is your friend okay? Gracie's sweet little voice sounded from the darkness.

"Gracie? Are you here?"

A small apparition appeared standing beside a headstone with a schnauzer inscribed in its surface. Gracie's curly hair fell loosely over her shoulders as it must have been when she'd crossed over. Starling gasped. She'd only seen a spirit in solid, or rather smoky, form the day her mother had been killed—the day that she had seen Asclepius for the first time and when he had begun his maddening quest for her to find the books.

"Do you know why I can see you?" she asked, trying to sound calm about addressing a little girl who looked exactly like her stone memorial.

"I don't know," Gracie said, her voice suddenly more than a ghostly whisper. It sounded as if the girl truly stood in front of her. "Do you think your gift is growing stronger?"

Stronger … was that it? Or rather, was it a stress induced gift of sight? Only time would tell.

"Gracie, I need to find the books. They have to be back in the mausoleum where Jasper was possessed. Would you please show me the quickest way to get there?"

Gracie nodded. She moved away from the headstone and a small apparition of a dog came out of the ground and followed as she moved quickly through the labyrinth of markers. The schnauzer twisted around the girl's feet, happily prancing as it gazed lovingly up at Gracie. Starling had to hold her purse steady as she jogged to keep up with the duo.

The faster the better—Bethany probably had more than her fair share of henchman who could be ready to kidnap Starling, or worse, at a moment's notice.

She couldn't be taken by Bethany or Edward again. They were even more dangerous than the Catharterians. As she followed Gracie under a Spanish moss laden oak, the archangel came into view. Her hands were up, once again ready to receive.

Gracie and the dog stopped beside the statue, practically standing on the name, Avi Mortem. A third apparition took form beside them.

This time you must do what you know is right or another person you love will be lost. As the apparition became clearer, Asclepius's voice strengthened, moving from a spectral whisper to the realm of reality, just as Gracie's had. "It's so nice to be with you," he said with a slight bow of his head. His beard was longer than the last time she'd seen him, or maybe it was just her memory playing tricks on her. Yet, the fine lines around his eyes and his godlike face remained the same.

"Will you go in with me? I could use your help in finding the books. I don't have a clue where to start looking, and Bethany's men are coming any minute."

"Starling, Gracie and I can't go into that terrible place. If the Catharterians catch us, they will be able to entrap our souls just as they did with Edward." Asclepius stepped closer and rested his milky hand on her shoulder, his icy touch making her shiver. "You have to go alone, but I'll be here ready to protect you."

"I don't want Gracie to get hurt."

Asclepius smiled, giving him a fatherly look. "Don't worry about little Gracie. I'll help her. I think you'd be surprised; she is far tougher than she looks." He glanced over at the cherubic-faced girl. "Just because she was young when she passed doesn't mean that she hasn't learned a few tricks of the ghostly trade."

"Gracie, if I get the books, I'll help you cross to the other side." Starling tried to say it with a reassuring smile, but it was hard to reassure the girl when so many things could go wrong. Gracie gave her a small nod as she patted the dog's head.

"Run along," Asclepius continued, "we'll be here waiting."

A tight knot formed in her stomach. "And if something happens to me, promise me that you will save Jasper. Okay?" She tried to tell herself that she was overreacting, but the souls' sudden appearance made her realize exactly how much danger surrounded her.

"You will save him yourself. You must." Asclepius pointed at the archangel's hand. "Now push the button and hurry. They are coming."

Starling slipped her fingers over the angel's palm, feeling around the night-chilled stone. She pressed the button and repeated the words she had said only hours before. "Avi Mortem, find comfort in the arms of the wicked and solace where no other dares. Mortem. Genus. Honor."

The angel's wings parted.

The scent of wet earth swirled up from the darkness as she descended into the cavernous maw of the mausoleum. If she never spent another moment in a graveyard, it would be a moment too soon. Everything about this place reminded her of her mother and the impermanence of everything in her life—even demigods like she and her mother. Even with their near immortality, death lingered over them like a dark cloud, threatening not only them, but the men that they loved—all thanks to Zeus and his curse.

Her footsteps echoed around her. At least she would be able to hear someone coming—that was, if they were alive.

Reaching the bottom of the steps, she turned on her cell phone light and pointed it around the rectangular room. A thin layer of dust covered the seats of two chairs by the door, but the dust in a wash basin had been disturbed; fingerprints smudged the concrete surface, but it was hard to tell if the fingerprints were Jasper's or someone else's—one of the "bad ones."

The door to the back room opened with a shrill squeak. If there was anyone down here, the sound would have surely warned them of her presence. But she was met with only the thundering of her own heartbeat and the loudness of her breath.

There had been many times she'd been afraid in her life: when her mother had died, when she found out she was a nymph, and when she learned she would have to live with Chance and Harper. It surprised her that now, when so much depended on a high-stake game of hide-and-go-seek that she was no longer troubled; instead, she was determined.

Opening the door wide, she made her way into the next room. The light of her phone was swallowed by the heavy darkness, and instead of fighting it, she turned to her left. The dust crumbled under her fingertips as she felt her way along the wall. She moved ten steps before she came to the end.

You have no business being here. A woman's voice sounded from the abyss.

Starling pressed her body against the wall. Reaching in her purse, she pulled out the only weapon-like thing she possessed—a ballpoint pen.

What are you going to do with that—color me to death? The woman's laugh bounced off the walls like a rubber ball coming to rest at Starling's feet.

"Who are you?" She shined her phone's light out into the room, but she could see no one. If the woman was alone, Starling would have a chance, but she would be hard pressed to defend herself against any more.

I'm guessing you are Starling. I've been hearing about you.

Starling gripped the pen tighter in her hand as she tried to turn her body in the direction of the voice. "Are you a Catharterian?"

Far from it. I'm one of their captured souls.

"You're a ghost?" Did that mean that she was going to be invaded and possessed as Jasper had been? "Step into the light."

A woman with blonde bouffant hair stepped into the faint light of Starling's phone. She wore a pink poodle skirt and bobby socks straight out of the 1950s. The only thing that made it clear the woman wasn't alive were the muted hues of her clothes and the near transparency of her skin.

The woman curtsied. "Molly B. at your service."

Starling wasn't sure whether to run or to face the ghost. From the curtsy, she had to believe that the woman wasn't here to hurt her. Heck, if she'd wanted to, she could have already attacked when Starling was making her way into the room. But if Devon and Edward had taught her anything, it was not to trust.

"How do you know who I am?" Starling asked.

"My masters, the vultures, have been having meetings about you. The last one was just a few weeks ago, in this very room."

The darkened room seemed like the last place Starling would ever want to have a meeting, but somehow it seemed to fit the scavengers of death.

Molly drifted toward her, stopping just a few feet in front of her, and reaching out, she flicked on a light switch. The sudden brightness made Starling shield her eyes, allowing them a moment to adjust. In the center of the massive room was a large, solid rectangle of onyx with a vulture carved into its ink-black surface and surrounded by chairs. If it hadn't been her enemy's, it would have been easy to call it beautiful, but as it stood, the long meeting table only made bile rise in her throat.

"Are you going to tell them I'm here?"

Molly drifted toward the table, her back to Starling and her two-toned shoes hovering just above the cement floor. "Do you like being a nymph?" Molly asked, avoiding Starling's question.

"I don't really know. I haven't been a nymph for very long."

"You are the youngest of your kind, yes?"

She nodded, unsure of where the woman was leading with her questions.

"Do you think you will be able to have children?" the spirit asked, trailing her fingers down the black table.

"I dunno. I haven't really given that much thought."

"But you want children someday?"

"Yeah, maybe after I graduate from college."

Molly nodded appreciatively. "I wanted kids, too. Before I died."

Starling wasn't sure what to say. "I'm sorry."

"When I was alive, that was what was expected of women like me. Get done with school, marry off, have a few kids. It was the bee's knees."

Starling stood in silence, just watching as the woman made her way to the head of the table.

"You know that's what the vultures are after, don't you?" Molly stopped at the farthest end. "They want to be able to have children."

"I know. They told me all about it when they tried to kill my friend, Harper."

Molly studied her for a moment. "Why don't you want them to be able to have more of their kind?"

Starling struggled to find the right answer. Was Molly on their side? Or was this woman measuring her response for another reason? The ghost didn't seem like a threat, but Gracie had warned her that those who roamed here were the "bad ones."

Molly had yet to earn her trust.

"The vultures are responsible for my mother's death, and they tried to kill my friend. Do you think I should just give them what they need so they always kill to get what they want?"

"But once they get what they need, they won't have to kill. They won't need spirits like me anymore. Maybe they will let me take the next step in the afterlife. They will go back to being peaceful."

"Scavengers of death are never peaceful. They may go back to leaving us alone, but what happens to the nymphs when they decide they need something again? We can't be bullied by their group." Starling gripped her pen tighter, letting it strengthen her resolve to say what needed to be said. "These creatures are the worst kind of bullies, and the only way to stop a bully is to put your foot down. They're lucky I'm not the kind to go after payback—that I'm satisfied that my mother's killer has found justice. I have every right to take down their entire group for what they've done to me and my kind."

"You know they won't stop until they get what they need," Molly said, flattening her skirt. "They're desperate. And desperation drives people to extreme lengths. I mean, just look at you. Here you are, coming back to the one place you should be running away from. Either you have a death wish or you are desperate. The only question is, which is it?"

"Is that some kind of threat?" Starling glanced around the room to see if there was another way to escape besides the door she'd entered through, but found none.

Molly laughed. "I don't want to hurt you. I just want to know why you came back. If anything, I look up to you. I saw what happened to your friend. It had to take a whole lot of gumption to come down here after that."

Gumption. That was one thing she had, but gumption didn't get her the books. It always seemed to dig her deeper into trouble.

"But why did you do it when the Catharterians could be here any second?" Molly continued.

"Because I need answers. And I think that there's a set of books down here that could carry exactly that."

"You talkin' about the *Libros*?"

Starling dropped her pen into her purse. "You know them? Where are they?"

"Whoa. Don't get excited. I only know about those books because they used the enchantments from it to trap me down here a few months back."

"They used it to trap you? What else can they do with the books?"

"Anything they want. Even erase a soul." Molly pulled out the chair and sat down, carefully crossing her ankles. "And that's why I wanted to talk to you."

"Do you think they are going to erase my soul? Will they erase yours? Will they erase Jasper's?"

Molly answered with a slow nod. "If they find Edward, they will get Jasper, and then they will come after me. Any time anything goes wrong, they always threaten us. And this thing with Edward, this running off, may push them over the edge. I just have to hope that they will show mercy."

"Look, Molly. I would love to help you—I would give anything to stop you from being hurt—but I can't do anything without the books. If they used spells from them, maybe I can, too. If you want me to help you, you need to tell me anything you know about them."

"The books are near. I know that, but I couldn't tell you where. I'm not usually allowed in this room; this is Edward's place. The spells confined us to these two rooms, but I normally stayed in the antechamber."

"If the books are down here, there's not that many places they could hide. There are only two rooms. We can chisel the entire thing apart to get those books."

"Not everything is as it looks," Molly said, pushing away the chairs that surrounded the table. She knocked on the surface of the onyx table. "I've seen this a few times, but I have no idea how it works."

"What are you doing?"

Molly bent down, inspecting the side of the table. "There's a button somewhere around here. I've seen them push it."

"Stop. What happens if you push the button?"

Molly barely looked up from her search. "It's fine. It's an elevator. The table goes down and then they come up."

"From where?"

"Down there. They always enter through the elevator."

"What's *down there*?" Starling asked. She shuddered as she envisioned a labyrinth full of death-fed vultures, the walls filled with the bones of their victims—a catacomb visage of their carnage.

"How am I supposed to know? Now stop asking me questions and help me find the button."

Starling crossed the room and as she approached Molly, the table began to shift and a low whirring sound filled the room. "You found it?"

Molly looked up at her, her eyes wide. "No. They're coming."

No. Sprinting, Starling made her way out the door and into the antechamber. There was a loud thump as the elevator must have come to a stop.

A woman's voice escaped the conference room. "We should've never trusted that idiot, Edward. At least we won't have to worry about him anymore. But it will be a trick to find Starling. You have men posted outside of her hotel, yes?"

"Yes, ma'am," a man with a familiar southern drawl answered. "We'll find her. She won't leave the city without her lover. As long as we have Jasper in custody—or what's left of him—she'll have reason to stay. In fact, she'll come to us."

She froze. They had Jasper in custody.

"What did you do with the Voodoo Queen?" the woman asked.

"Let's just say she will have to learn to do her charms and whatnot with one hand. We needed to send a message—no one goes against the council."

"Good ... And you took the man to headquarters?"

Starling held her breath as she listened.

"Yes, Ms. Virginia."

There was a squeak of a chair and a groan as someone must have sat down.

There was no possible way she would just give herself over to them. Starling tiptoed up the stairs.

"Molly, why are the lights on in here?" the woman asked the ghost.

She tried not to think of what would happen if the ghost ratted her out. Would the Catharterians kill her? Or would they use her to get to the Sisterhood—or worse?

Getting to the top step, she stopped. The angel's wings had closed behind her. Running her fingers over the marble, she searched for a button or a switch, anything that would open the wings so she could escape. There was nothing.

How had Edward gotten out?

Gracie? Asclepius? Can you hear me? She silently pleaded.

There was no answer.

Maybe she could call someone. Jamie would help her. Starling grabbed her phone and, covering the light so no one would see the glow, glanced at the screen. No service.

"Molly, answer me. Why were the lights on in this room?" the woman repeated.

Starling tried to swallow back her panic as the voices grew louder.

I'm sorry, Ms. Virginia, I was lonely. Now that Edward's gone, the darkness was just too much.

Some of her panic retreated thanks to the ghost's loyalty. "Get used to being without Edward. We erased him. And if you continue to disobey our rules, we'll erase you. You are here to guard this place—if you touch anything, it will be the last thing you ever do," the woman threatened. "Do you understand?"

There was a weighted pause. "Yes, ma'am," Molly answered.

"You need to leave. Now," Virginia ordered.

Starling ran her hands down the rough concrete walls but still couldn't find a button. The ghosts who waited for her outside the wings couldn't press the button in the angel's hand. There was only one thing left to try.

"Avi Mortem, find comfort in the arms of the wicked and solace where no other dares. Mortem. Genus. Honor," Starling whispered the incantation.

Nothing happened.

She was trapped in a grave with her enemies.

Chapter Thirteen

Jasper's head ached and his face was swollen around his left eye. If he'd only been more careful, he would have never been possessed. None of this would have happened. He'd been stupid. They never should have gone after those damn books. There had be another way to save Starling from the spirits—something far less dangerous.

He glanced around the small room. The walls were made of corrugated steel, almost like he was in some kind of shed. He tried to move his limbs, but the restraints were tied around his chair, and as he struggled, the rope only cut deeper into his wrists and ankles.

"Don't try it," a man said, pressing a cold, steel gun barrel into the side of his neck.

Jasper turned his head to look at the man. He was heavyset and graying, with eyes that reminded him of an angry rat. Something about him was familiar, but Jasper didn't recognize him.

"What is this place?" Jasper asked, as he leaned away from the cold steel.

The man relaxed his pressure on the gun. "You're nowhere."

"Where did Edward go? Is he coming back?" The last thing Jasper remembered was being hit in the face with sand. After that, everything had gotten a little fuzzy. There had been people, blood, chanting, and then no more Eddie.

The man laughed. "He's been erased. But if you miss your little friend, I'm sure we could find another spirit. From what I've seen of ya, it would be an improvement."

Asshole.

"What does *erased* mean?"

"Let's just say he won't possess anyone or anything ever again. But that's what you get when you go against the council."

The council. Jasper cringed. Being possessed was bad enough, but here he was a prisoner of the one organization he'd been trying to investigate. Well, at least his investigation was over. He could tell the Sisterhood he'd found them. That was, if he made it out of this shit alive. First things first—he needed to find Starling. He'd already failed her once by allowing himself to be taken down by a ghost. He couldn't fail again.

"Do you know who I am?" the man asked, a smug grin crossing his face.

"I know you're an asshole."

"Wrong." The man drove the gun deeper into the side of Jasper's neck. "I'm not surprised you don't remember me, but you and I met at the bank, and then I saw you in your cab earlier today. Things like that I don't forget, but I guess a guy like you—one so wrapped up in being Prince Charming for his little wench—wouldn't remember an old man like me."

Ah, yes. The man who'd introduced them to Devon, the same man who had crossed the street in front of them when they'd first arrived at the cemetery. Why hadn't he recognized him? Was the man right, had he been so focused on Starling that he'd missed important details? "Was the man in the black SUV with you, too?"

"He's one of Walter's men. You'll get a chance to meet some more of our faction when I take you back to headquarters."

Back to headquarters? A few weeks ago, Jasper would have jumped at the chance to infiltrate their offices and learn about the faction inside their organization for the Sisterhood, but now with Starling at risk, it was the last place he wanted to be. Yet, it was still better than being possessed—it was easier to escape walls than it was to escape the grips of a malevolent spirit. No wonder Starling hated them so much.

"What's your name?"

The man's phone rang and he turned away from Jasper. "Yep," he answered.

There was a muffled reply from the other end.

"You got it," the man said, clicking off the phone. "Looks like you get to see a little more of Savannah."

"I've already seen enough."

"That's what your little girlfriend, Starling, said, too."

"You didn't touch her. If you did, I will kill you."

"She is a pretty little thing, isn't she?" The gray-haired man smirked, driving a stake into Jasper's heart. "I'm looking forward to getting the chance to breed with her."

"What the fuck are you talking about?"

"Oh, you haven't heard?" the man asked, driving the stake deeper. "Virginia has decided if we can't get our hands on the drugs, we will have to do the next best thing. We can't have our kind dying off. It's better to have little half-breeds than nothing at all."

Jasper tugged at his hands, trying desperately to free them. The rough rope dug deeper into his wrists and the blood wetted his skin.

"Now, I don't normally agree with our little commingling, but that was until I saw you two at the bank. That woman's hotter than any watermelon queen. I haven't seen tits like that in a long time. I bet you love them. Too bad you won't get to see them puppies again." The man whistled through his front teeth. "I heard if you lick a nymph's nipple, it tastes like honey. Is it true?"

"Shut up. Don't you dare touch her."

"Haven't you gotten a chance at it yet?" The man inspected his fingernails. He looked up, his gaze threatening. "If you're still alive when I get done, I'll let you know how sweet they taste."

"You dirty mother … You wouldn't dare," Jasper threatened as he tried to flail against his chest and leg restraints. "You and your kind don't deserve to live."

The man's backhand connected with his already puffy left cheek. Iron-flavored blood poured into his mouth. "You are dead." He spit the blood onto the man's black penny loafers.

"I'm really afraid." The man took a handkerchief and wiped the blood from his shoe. He wiped his fingers clean, balled up the fabric, and stuffed it into Jasper's mouth.

The man would have no easy death.

• • •

Midnight. The sounds of the voices in the conference room had started to quiet, growing so faint, it was difficult for Starling to hear from the top of the steps. She tiptoed down the stairs, careful to make no sound as she descended.

"Did you call him?" the woman in charge asked someone.

"He'll meet us in the main hall."

"Now all we have to do is find a little more bait." There was a *whir* as the elevator must have clicked to life. "Devon, are you coming?"

Devon was a Catharterian? She should have known. He must have been the one to get into the safe deposit box and plant the feather. Had he also planted the note from Epione? Was her goddess working with the vultures? No. She wouldn't go against her own kind.

"Grab the book. The rest of the council will want it for the meeting. We need to get a handle on the situation with the girl. Time is against us—they killed another of our kind in Crete. The Sisterhood can't be allowed to grow ranks. They already outnumber us. We need more scions or soon there will be none of us left to continue our quest."

Their voices grew quieter and someone turned off the lights in the conference room, making the thin stream of light under the door disappear. Starling made her way to the door. She listened,

114

but there was nothing. "Molly, you here? Are they gone?" she whispered.

"They took one of the *Libros* with them." The ghost stepped through the closed door. "But I saw where they got the book. Come on, maybe the other books are in there."

"How many books are there?" Starling asked as she opened the door and flicked the lights back on in the conference room.

"As far as I can tell, there are three. Each has a different cover. There's the White—which they took—there's the Black and the Red." Molly drifted across the room to the far wall. "The good news is, I saw where they pushed the button to move the table. But the bad news is, there's no way to get the book without using the elevator."

The woman, whoever she was, had said the entire council was waiting. For all Starling knew, there could be hundreds of Catharterians down there. Then again, this could be the last opportunity to rid herself and the Sisterhood of the fear of the vultures.

"Where's the switch?" Starling caught up with the ghost and bent down to get on Molly's eye level.

There, on the underside of the table, was a tiny black button. It blended seamlessly into the table. Molly stood up. "There's also another one, right there," she said pointing to the ruby-colored eye of the carved vulture.

Starling stared at the bird's eye. She could press the buttons and descend into the unknown, maybe get the books, but most likely run into more vultures than she could handle. It was risky, but she had to help Jasper. They had him. And there was no telling what they would do to him to get at her.

Jasper had once told her that an enemy was most dangerous when he held secrets. Having heard their secrets, she had an advantage and could turn the battle in her favor. They wanted to bring her to them using Jasper, but they weren't ready. The only time to act was now.

"Push the buttons. We need to get down there."

"But what if they are just outside the doors?" Molly challenged. "There's no way you will be able to defend yourself."

"I'm not worried about me. I'm worried about Jasper. If I don't do something, they are going to kill him."

"If they get their hands on you, they may well kill you. Then you both die. Think it through."

Starling paused. Molly was right, but that didn't mean she could stop now, when she was so close to Jasper and perhaps the books.

"Are there any more of your kind here?"

Molly shook her head. "It was only Edward and me."

"Can you talk to the ghosts in the rest of the cemetery?"

"No. This ground carries a spell. No spirits in, no spirits out."

Crap. There was no getting out of this trap. The only help she would get would be from the ghost at her side.

"Do you think you could go below?" Starling tapped the table.

Molly sighed. "I'd love to try. Anything has to be better than staying in this place. I can't tell you how tired I am of these two rooms and those who keep me here."

"I bet you are." Starling turned to face the ghost. "By the way, thank you for not giving me up to the vultures. I know you could have bartered me for your freedom."

"It was nothing. It's the first time I've really gotten to help anyone since I died."

"It wasn't nothing. You gave up everything and I truly appreciate it. There are only a handful of people in my life who would have done something like that for me. I promise if we get those books, I will find a way to help you escape this prison they've created for you. You deserve so much more."

" I don't know about that … I've made my share of mistakes.

"We've all made mistakes." Just like she had in leaving Jasper behind in the voodoo shop. "And it seems I just keep making more."

"My momma always said the thing about mistakes is that we must learn from them and keep moving forward. We can't help anyone if we are burdened by the weight of our past. I can't say I've always listened, but maybe you will."

What a thought—to not let her mistakes be a burden. It was a wonderful thought, but how could she possibly let go of all the pain she had caused? Molly must have never gotten one person killed and another kidnapped. She couldn't possibly understand how much guilt Starling carried. Self-forgiveness wasn't an option.

"Right now I have to focus on Jasper. I can't let him get hurt more than he may already be." Starling pressed the button on the side of the table and reaching over, pressed the vulture's eye.

"Here's hoping we can get to him in time."

The elevator whirred to life and the table shifted under her fingers. Starling stepped back and watched as the table rose, exposing a small two-person lift. Set into the wall, next to the lift's door, was a small cabinet nestled in the protected space between that door and the edge of the table. "Is that where Devon got the book?" Starling asked, motioning toward the box.

Molly nodded. "I think so."

Starling stepped in the small elevator; Molly drifted in beside her.

"I hope this works," Molly said. "I've tried moving through the floors, but couldn't."

Starling's stomach churned at the thought of going through the Catharterians' headquarters alone. "I need you."

Molly reached to pat Starling's cheek, but Starling could feel nothing except a cold draft against her skin. "Thank you. It's been a long time since anyone told me something so sweet. Edward wasn't one much for company."

"Do you think you'd want to stay as a ghost, or would you rather completely cross?" Starling opened the cabinet where the book had rested. The box in the elevator was empty. She wasn't surprised, but a deep disappointment crept through her. Nothing ever seemed to come easy.

"I think I would cross over." Molly glanced up at the earthen ceiling of the mausoleum. "It would be nice to see my family again. I would like to think they'd be happy to see me, especially my momma. The last time I saw her was the day of my services."

Starling shut the door and pressed the down button. "I'm sure she'll be waiting for you. Just like mine will be waiting for me someday …"

"But you're a nymph—doesn't that mean you will never have to cross over?"

The elevator started slowly before gradually picking up speed. "We can cross over. We are not gods, only demigods. We have a weakness that can result in death. The truth is that it is easy to forget sometimes that we are vulnerable. My mother did, but maybe if she hadn't thought she was almost invincible, she would've run instead of faced her killer."

"It sounds like your mother was very brave …" Molly's voice quieted as they moved deeper into the earth. Starling glanced over at her friend. Her frost-white wraith started to fade and rise in the air. "I believe that now it is your time. The mausoleum is pulling me back. I can't go … You must be brave."

"Molly!" She reached out, but as she moved, Molly disappeared. "Molly!"

Her fear grew as the elevator steadily moved downward. She was alone. But Molly had been right—now was the time to be brave.

Chapter Fourteen

Starling sucked in a breath as the door of the elevator opened. She gripped her purse tight as the room came into view. It wasn't the catacombs that she had imagined; instead the walls were covered in pictures of men in the powdered wigs of days long gone; farther down were more recent pictures, some of women with beehives and others of men with bushy sideburns. Nameplates were mounted to the wall beneath each. The closest to her read: Colonel Redbird 1803-1865, Killed in Action.

She found it hard to believe that the man in the picture—the overstuffed, bird-beaked man—would have died fighting. He was a vulture. More than likely, he would have been out in the fields making quick work of the dead while he fed on their souls. Just like his current counterparts would do if they found her gawking in their hall.

She rushed through the room. The staccato of her footsteps filled the empty space. There was a door to her right and she stopped to listen for sound. Inside, a man was talking.

His voice was harsh and thick. "I can't agree to this plan. She is an innocent. What kind of message are we sending to others if we start killing and maiming those who have done us no harm?"

"You didn't seem to have a problem sending your man to beat Jasper."

Starling reached for the door handle, ready to tell the man off for hurting her friend, but she stopped. The only way she could help Jasper now was by finding him.

"That was different and you know it. He's been investigating us for months. He is an enemy. Starling is nothing more than a pawn."

"We must carry a big stick, Walter," a woman answered, and her voice was familiar—in fact, it was the same voice from the conference room of the mausoleum. "If we show that we are weak, we will be taken down. It's survival of the fittest. You know that as well as I do."

"Taking a girl and keeping her against her will isn't strength—it's a felony. I want no part of what you are planning. If you keep her here for any other reason than to barter for the drugs, I will leave this group—and take my men with me."

"You made a vow. I helped you with your troubles when you needed me, and now when our entire species is at risk, you threaten me? We don't need your men. It is fine by me if you and your line die off. It will guarantee that only those who have a true heart, a heart that cares about what is important, will pass on their genes."

Footsteps approached the door, forcing Starling to hurry down the hall, until she came to the next doorway. She paused for a moment. A new fear rose. From what she'd heard, it sounded as if they didn't want just the drugs—they wanted her. But for what?

The door suddenly smashed against the wall. "We are leaving, Virginia. This, and you, are crazy. Good luck fulfilling your agenda without my support. I never should have gone against the president."

"Stop, Walter. I'm sorry. Maybe we can figure something out."

"You can't force her to carry our line. Do you understand me?"

"Deal. But we will need her for a little while to conduct research."

"You can't destroy her."

"Walter, we will try to keep her alive, but I can't make that promise."

"Goddamn, Virginia, you made a vow when you became vice president—you promised this shit would come to a stop, but you have only cost us more lives and more heartache. You never had any intention of using your office for good; you wanted to use it only for your own ends."

"Go to hell."

"I would, but I'm afraid I would meet you there." The door banged shut.

Starling frantically opened the door to the room and slipped inside so the defecting man wouldn't see her and turn her over to Virginia. She needed him to leave. One enemy was easier to fight than two.

She sighed with relief as the sound of Walter's angry footsteps cascaded down the hall. She clicked the door shut and turned toward the room.

Sitting in the center of the wood-paneled room was a single chair. A man was slumped over in the seat, his hands tied to the armrests. He didn't move as she approached. The man's dark hair was matted with dried blood.

"Sir?" she whispered. "Sir, are you okay?"

The man groaned and shook as he looked up. A trail of dried blood cracked on his cheek and his eye was swollen and black. Jasper peered at her, his eyes lighting up when he recognized her. "Starling? I'm so glad you're here."

"Oh my God." Starling gasped. "What did they do to you, Jasper?"

"I'm fine," he said with a stuttering exhale. He tried to laugh, but it ended in a wince. "Some guy roughed me up and brought me here. And then Devon decided I was still too good looking."

Chapter Fifteen

He had never been so happy to see a friendly face, and not just any friendly face, but Starling's. She was absolutely radiant in her fury. Her cheeks were flushed and her eyes were filled with fire.

"These goddamn birds. I will kill every last one of them for this," she growled as she started to untie the rope from his aching wrist. "What happened to you?"

"Some old guy brought me here. He got the drop on me when Edward was in control." He paused for a moment as he drew in a long painful breath. "After they brought me here, they let Devon have a go."

"I'm so sorry, Jasper. I shouldn't have had anything to do with him." Starling released his right hand. With his free hand, he reached over to untie the other while Starling moved to his ankle.

"It wasn't your fault. You didn't know he was in league with the vultures."

"True, but I knew he was an asshole. Maybe if I hadn't gone to the piano bar with him, or maybe if I hadn't introduced you to him, then he wouldn't have gone after you so badly." She untied the last bit of rope from his ankle and then reached up for his face. Her thumb brushed over his cheek. The warmth of her touch drew sparks of desire to the front of his mind. She'd never touched him like that before. Never with such *tenderness*.

No. Everything was so screwed up. Maybe she cared for him, but she couldn't feel anything more. Then again, he couldn't say the same. For the last few months, every minute of his life had been spent thinking about ways to protect her and keep her safe. She was the first thought on his mind when woke and the last thought before he fell asleep. But damn it, that didn't mean he loved her, did it? Not to mention her curse—the nymph's curse. If he fell in love with her, he was fated to die.

She reached up with her other hand and placed it on his cheek. "I'm so sorry, Jasper. I just can't say it enough. This is all my fault." Tears welled in her eyes, and seeing her hurt for him made his pain suddenly worsen.

He reached up and put his hands over hers. "It's okay, Starling. This was my choice. I knew what I was getting into when I took on the job of guarding you. I'm sorry I failed. I really fucked up. Look at us now in the enemy's headquarters. I'm hurt. We're trapped. And … wait … " He gripped her fingers. "Are you here because of me?"

She looked away from his gaze.

"You are." He ran his thumbs over the back of her hands. "I can't believe you put yourself in danger."

"We're a team, remember? You tried to help me, now it's my turn to help you."

He ran his hands up her arm until the warmth of her neck called to him, making him want to lean in and kiss her soft skin. "How did you get in here?"

"Through the mausoleum. There was an entrance in the table in the backroom."

"Do they know you're here?"

She shook her head. "If we hurry maybe we can go back the way I came."

He moved toward her, focusing on the soft, pink line of her lips. He pressed his lips against hers. Her lips were sweet as they moved against his then opened slightly, inviting his kiss to deepen, awakening his body to more carnal needs. He went hard. He pulled her up and into his lap. She moaned into his mouth as her body pressed against his.

He broke away from their kiss. It had to stop. He couldn't feel this—this need, this want, or this insatiable hunger for her touch.

"You shouldn't have come to help me, Starling." He sighed, trying to gain control over his body.

"I didn't come down here just for you." Her gaze met his, her beautiful blue eyes sparkling—was it anger? Or something else? "The books are down here, too." She stood up and away from his lap; the heat of where she rested turned cold.

So he hadn't been the reason she'd broken into the headquarters. He should have been relieved, but disappointment drifted through him.

"Do you know where?" he asked, trying to concentrate on something other than his feelings.

"No idea, but if we're together I'm sure we can find them and then get out of here."

The door to the room opened. "In such a rush to go already?" A woman stood in the doorway, her arms crossed over her chest. She reached down, pulled a satellite phone from her back pocket, and dialed.

A man's garbled voice answered.

"We got her. They're in the torture room. Meet me here. Bring Jim."

The man said something and Virginia's face puckered.

"Walter and his men won't be joining us. Now, get on it."

Jasper stood up and started to move toward the woman.

"Stop. Right. There." The woman pulled a gun from her belt. "You aren't going anywhere." She slid the phone back into her pocket.

He stopped. "Who the fuck are you?"

"I'm Virginia, the vice president of the Catharterian Council."

"The vice president? I didn't know that there was a vice president of shitheads," he retorted.

Virginia glanced over at Starling, ignoring his jibe. "I'm so glad you have decided to join us. Thanks for saving us the work of finding you."

"Screw you," Starling snapped.

"Wow, I was hoping we could get things started on a better footing. We have quite a bit we need to go over with you. If you choose to make this difficult, then it could be quite disastrous to your health."

"You aren't going to do shit," he said, stepping protectively in front of Starling. "You won't touch her."

"You're right there, Jasper. *I* have no interest in touching your little *friend*, but I do want what she carries. Do you have the GX 149 with you?" she demanded of Starling.

Starling glanced at him, her eyes wide with fear. "I'm not giving you the drugs. You and your kind don't deserve to breed after what you did to my mother and then tried to do to Harper."

"What gives you the right to say what we do and don't deserve, girl?" Virginia's stoicism crumbled. "You're too young to know the value of children. The joy they bring to a parent's life."

"You are manipulative, uncaring, and power-hungry. You don't have a motherly bone in your body. There has to be something more." Starling paused. "Why do you really want to have children?"

"You barely know me. I don't know what gives you the impression I wouldn't be a good mother," Virginia said, the lines in her face pulled tightly.

"I heard you and Devon in the mausoleum. I know who you really are."

"You don't know the half of it, Starling. Virginia is so full of shit," he said. "You don't want children because you love them, or you want to become a mother. You want children so you can build an army."

"How do you know?" Starling asked.

"Devon was more than happy to supplement my beating with tales of how a new generation of vultures would help earn them impressive military titles in the future," he said.

"Come now, you two little lovebirds," Virginia said dismissively, but there was a flash of shock in her eyes that confirmed his little jab was, indeed, her secret. "Why would *we* want an army?"

"I don't know," Jasper said. "But I will find out."

"Is that right?" Virginia smiled wickedly.

The door to the room opened. Devon sauntered in and passed Jasper a smug grin. "Can't say I'm happy to see you again, man."

The hairs on the back of Jasper's neck rose. "Don't worry. We won't be staying long."

"That's not what I heard," Devon said. His gaze strayed over Starling, landed on her chest, and moved down to the intersection of her thighs.

They needed to get out of here and Virginia was clearly the one with the power, and therefore the most important to outsmart. "Look, if we agree to give you Starling's drugs, then you let us go. Deal?"

Virginia laughed. "So now you are ready to make deals, when you are our prisoner and you have no way to escape? You have no leg to stand on. No deal. We will just take what we want."

"No, you won't," Starling said, gripping her purse tighter to her body.

"You want me to get them, Ms. Virginia?" Devon motioned toward Starling's bag.

Virginia nodded. Devon reached for Starling's bag, pulling it from her shoulder. Starling grabbed the straps, trying in vain to keep her property from falling into the hands of the Catharterians. It reminded Jasper of when he'd picked her up in Savannah. Unfortunately, this time he wouldn't be able to rescue her or her bag.

"Just give him the bag, honey," Jasper said, touching her hand.

Starling let go, but there was hurt in her eyes as he forced her to give up. "I need my medication."

"No, Starling, you don't. We will *find* something else. I promise," Jasper hinted. "Besides, there aren't very many pills in your purse, are there?"

Some of the hurt was replaced with a flicker of excitement as she must have realized they still had a maneuver left in their arsenal.

"You're right. I only brought enough GX 149 for a few days."

That was his girl. He shouldn't have doubted that she would catch his clues and run with it.

"I don't think that would be long enough for it to really affect fertility. Maybe we could make some kind of deal for inventory back in Vegas? You can have the rest of my drugs if you let Jasper and I go and promise to never bother another nymph again."

He couldn't help but feel proud of Starling as she stood there—strong, confident, and powerful, defying her enemies.

"We don't want just the drugs. We want the formula as well," Virginia said. "More than that, we need proof the drugs will work. Until we have a pregnancy in our population, you will have to stay here." The words dripped from her lips like putrid waste.

"No," Jasper interrupted. "You're crazy if you think I'm going to let you keep her here."

"Virginia," Starling interrupted, "even if I wanted to help, I don't have the formula. That is in the hands of Harper and her team of pharmacologists."

"Devon, get Harper on the phone. Tell her that we will kill her stepdaughter if she doesn't get her ass here in the next twenty-four hours. Then take Starling and Jasper to their rooms."

"To our rooms?" Starling echoed.

"Would you rather stay in our dungeon?" Virginia asked. "We aren't complete animals. You've shown that you are willing to help us. However, if things change, or if you attempt to escape, our little bit of hospitality will no longer be an option. Do we have an understanding?"

Starling nodded.

"Good night. Spend it praying that Harper will come to your rescue. Otherwise, we will have to kill her to send not only you, but your Sisterhood a message."

They wouldn't kill Harper. They couldn't. She was well protected within her and Chance's new apartment in the Bellagio. Jasper had made sure of it over the last few months. Yet, Harper loved Starling. He had to assume that she would put herself at risk again.

"Let's go," Devon said, grabbing Starling by the arm and shoving her toward the open door.

"Don't touch her like that," Jasper growled. "If you do that again, I will personally cut off your hands and stick them where the sun doesn't shine."

"How you gonna do that, man? I don't see you packing a lot of heat." Devon laughed. "One helluva Sisterhood you must have there, darlin', to send in a bodyguard who can't even protect you. It's almost like they were hoping you would get killed. What did you do to piss them off?"

Starling shot him a pleading look, but there was nothing he could do—at least not now.

"Jasper, let's go," Virginia said, motioning for him to follow. She led him out of the room, through the main hall and into a maze of concrete-walled rooms and white halls. Right and then right again, finally a left. With each turn, Jasper's suspicion grew. Where were they really taking him? He had to find a weapon. Anything to take the vultures down and get the hell out of there, but every room they passed through was empty or nearly so, with a few only holding folded tables or large recliners. He realized how alone they were; they hadn't passed or seen even another vulture. Something was very, very wrong.

They made their way to a large atrium where the ceiling was painted to look like a morning sky, the mural reminding him of the Venetian in Las Vegas. The room had three long rows of rectangular tables, as if it was used for a meeting hall or cafeteria. He drew in a long breath. His sense of smell was weak, but he picked up hints of barbeque mixed with heady aroma of beer. The vultures must have fed on something more than death to sustain their bodies.

Sitting at the far end of the room was a small group of women. One of them looked up at the sound of the door closing behind the foursome.

"Ms. Virginia, I'm sorry," the woman said, standing up. The other women followed her lead. "We didn't know she had arrived." She motioned toward Starling. "Does the president know she is here?"

"Shut up," Virginia ordered. "Leave now and tell no one who or what you have seen."

Suddenly it made sense. Virginia hadn't been trying to get him lost in the maze of hallways and rooms. She was hiding them. But why was Virginia trying to sneak them through headquarters without the president's knowledge?

Devon pushed Starling forward, hustling her out of the dining hall. "Let's go."

"What's going on?" Jasper asked as he followed Starling. "Why are you hiding us? What are you doing?"

"If you don't shut up, I will kill you, man," Devon growled.

"Devon, stop," Virginia ordered. "I'm sure Jasper knows what is at risk—it's not just his life at stake."

"Tell me what the hell is going on," Jasper ordered. "Obviously you don't want your president to know we're here, but why?"

"I have no idea what you are talking about," Virginia said with a fake smile. "We simply want to get you into your rooms before we announce your arrival. After that, perhaps you will have a meeting with him."

He heard the words coming out of her mouth, but something about the way she spoke, or perhaps it was the way her body stiffened, made his suspicion rise.

Devon stopped in front of a long row of doors. "This is our dormitory area. Thanks to Walter, there's a suite that was recently vacated. You can put them in his old room. You'll be staying here, Starling." Taking a set of keys from his pocket, he unlocked the door.

The door opened to a large bedroom. Pictures of circling vultures adorned the walls. In the center of the room was a white queen-sized bed with Starling's luggage beside it. "We took the liberty of collecting your things from your hotel."

"You bastard. You had no right touching my things." Starling rushed into the room and lifted her bag onto the bed.

"We had a courier pick up your items. I was trying to make you more comfortable. It's hard to say how long you may be staying with us."

Starling blanched. "If I have my way, it won't be for more than one night."

Devon laughed. Virginia silenced him with a motion of her hand. "We shall see how cooperative you and Jasper are. In fact, if you play nicely, you may end up walking away from this experience."

He found that hard to believe. If they were hiding them, even if that meant putting them in the headquarters' nicest bedrooms, there was only a slight chance Starling would make it out alive—and an even smaller chance of his survival. No matter how he played through the possible scenarios in his head, for the vultures, he was expendable—or worse, a liability. In fact, if he were separated from Starling now, there was little chance that he would make it through the night.

He had to stay alive for her.

"She can't stay here alone. I won't allow it," he said, as he stopped beside Starling. "I don't trust you."

"That isn't a choice you get to make, Jasper," Virginia replied.

"Don't underestimate me," he threatened. "We can continue being the perfect little hostages, or we can start fighting. Your call."

Devon glanced over at Virginia. "We'd only have to run one guard during the night. It would draw less attention."

"Fine," Virginia conceded. "But if something goes wrong, Devon, I will personally take it out on you."

Jasper suddenly had an urge to make sure something went very wrong. He couldn't help but laugh.

"Something funny?" Devon grumbled.

"Not at all. I just imagined your face uglier than it already is. I really think you would have to start wearing a bag over your head."

Devon took a threatening step toward him, but Virginia stopped him. "No, Devon," she said, glancing down at her watch. "We only have a few hours before the council meets. We need to get our story together. There's no way, after we were seen in the dining hall, that we won't have a fight on our hands. We have to tie up a few loose ends before word spreads."

Devon nodded. "Got it, Ms. Virginia."

Virginia glared at Jasper. "As for you two, stay out of trouble. Your lives depend on your cooperation."

Chapter Sixteen

Starling rifled through her suitcase. She had all of her paperwork, her clothes, but the small, extra bottle of pills she had brought with her was missing. She had nothing left to trade for their freedom.

Jasper's face was tight and his brow furrowed. Even from across the room, she could hear him grind his teeth. He was a good bodyguard, but she couldn't imagine how he could get them out of this mess.

"You okay, Jasper?" she asked, pulling the zipper closed on her bag. She sat down on the edge of the bed, and as she stopped moving she realized exactly how exhausted she was. Even her eyes were tired.

"I'm fine. Are you okay?"

She nodded. Physically she was fine, but her emotions were a mess. There was no way they were going to be okay. On top of it all, she'd lost all of her medication and hadn't found the books. The only good thing about being down in the bowels of the Catharterian headquarters was that it kept the spirits at bay. So if she stayed here, she was a goner, but if she managed to get out of this place, freedom would be its own hell when the spirits inundated her once again. Regardless of what happened, a white picket fence, dog, and a normal life weren't in her future.

"You are being quiet." Jasper walked over and sat on the bed beside her.

"You're surprised that I'm quiet after everything we've been through? We are stuck in our enemy's headquarters. Nothing's going our way." It came as a shock, but she couldn't help the desire that simmered up from her core. Dark and dangerous—who knew that it could make a handsome man that much sexier? She looked away, focusing her attention on pushing her bag off the bed and onto the floor. It landed with a thump.

"At least we are together." Jasper picked her bag up off the floor and sat it on its pedestal legs. "I'm sorry about all of this, Starling. I could have stopped it all from happening if I'd been strong enough to ward off Edward's possession."

"Strength has nothing to do with it. You didn't stand a chance, Jasper. Once we get the books, maybe they'll have what we need to stop something like that from ever happening to you again."

"Do you know where we can find them?"

"Virginia took the White from the mausoleum, but I don't know where she was taking it. As for the other books, according to Molly, a ghost I met, there are two more books in the *Libros Umbrarum:* the Black and the Red."

"Did Molly know where to find them?" Jasper sat down on the edge of the bed, so close that he almost touched her.

The heat radiated off him, raising her desire from an ember to a flame. She couldn't feel this way toward him. He'd made it more than clear he had no interest in her. She was his to protect, not to love. She edged back into the headboard until she was sitting fully upright.

"She didn't." Starling tried not to stare at the painful looking cut under Jasper's eye.

"As far as I can tell, the headquarters is enormous. Even if we had weeks to search the place, I don't think there's much chance of us finding those books. That is, unless you can get some kind of clue where to look. Do you think you could use your powers?"

"You mean, do I think I could seduce someone to find out?"

"You can't tell me you haven't thought about it." Jasper looked down at his hands. "I don't understand why you don't. If I had a power like that ... " He shook his head. "Let's just say I would probably have more money and sex than would be healthy."

Anger trickled into the fire of her desire. "So you'd be a man whore?"

"Maybe in the past, but not now." Jasper looked over at her, and some of the darkness in his eyes disappeared, replaced by a flicker of something she couldn't quite place.

"Why not now?"

Jasper grinned, making his dimple more prominent. No matter how hard she tried to force back her feelings, she couldn't help the way her heart lifted along with the corners of his full, oh-so-kissable lips.

"Let's just say that life has a way of becoming complicated." He reached over and touched the back of her hand. His fingers stroked against her skin, intensifying her desire.

Did he know what he was doing? Did he understand what she experienced with just the thought of his lips pressed against hers again? If he did, he would have stopped. He would have been too protective to let her fall in love—even with him.

"How are we going to handle this, Jasper? How in the hell are we going to get out of here?"

"I don't know, but the longer we stay, the more likely it is that they will kill me and then probably you. I'm fine with dying for you, but I can't handle the thought that they are going to hurt you."

"Virginia isn't the first person who has wanted to hurt me and she's probably far from the last. If you haven't figured it out by now, Jasper, I'm a lot stronger than I look."

"And a lot more stubborn." He chuckled. "You don't want to underestimate her. She's hiding something, not only from us, but clearly from her council as well. You never know what a caged animal is willing to do to get what they want."

"So what are we going to do?"

"We need to find her Achilles' heel."

"Devon." Starling sighed as she glanced down at Jasper's fingers on hers. "He's her closest ally. If something happens to him, she will be down her right hand."

"That will only make her more reckless if we kill him."

"I'm not saying we kill him. I'm thinking that if I seduce him, he's our way to make it out of here alive. "

"So you're saying I was right about the whole seduction idea?"

"Right is a strong word," she said, running her thumb over his as she tried to memorize exactly how good it felt to have her hand in his. "I'm only saying that it wasn't such a bad idea. And right now, it is our only option. We don't have a whole lot of friends down here."

"No, but we have each other and we can make one helluva team." Jasper drew away his hand. "Just as long as we play it smart."

"Smart. Yeah." Starling nodded. She yearned for the return of his touch, anything to keep from thinking about the seduction that would have to come. Devon was an egotistical, chauvinistic leech who thought himself God's gift to women—and in a matter of hours he would be slobbering all over her.

"Where do you want me to sleep?" Jasper asked. "I'm more than happy to be on the floor, but I may need a blanket." He stood up. The place where his fingers had touched grew cool, and she could barely withstand the urge to reach out and pull him back to his place beside her.

"You can't sleep on the cold concrete. A man your age might not be able to stand up in the morning."

He answered with a playful growl. "You know I'm only a few years older than you. If I'm old, what are you?"

"I'm dignified," she said, faking a stuffy air as she straightened at the edge of her dirty red dress in an attempt to lighten the mood.

Jasper's laughter filled the room. It sounded so good to hear him laugh.

"Whatever you say. Just remember that I saw you trip over your own suitcase," he teased.

"That wasn't a trip, it was a defensive maneuver, and don't you forget it." There had been so much stress since he'd started once again being more than a shadow that she'd almost forgotten how good it felt to have a carefree moment, a moment of complete surrender. If only this moment could last forever.

"Oh I won't." His eyes sparkled.

"As far as tonight, you can sleep in the bed with me."

"Only if you promise to not use any of your *defensive* maneuvers," he pretended to grumble.

For a split second, she imagined his hand gliding over her skin, finding the curve of her thigh and sliding down. She shifted in the bed, making room for him on the other side. "Don't make me have to."

"Turn on the light," he said, pointing toward the lamp on the nightstand. "And I'll turn around for you to get changed."

She clicked on the light. "What are you going to wear?" She got out of bed and grabbed her bag. Unzipping the suitcase, she rifled through it. There was nothing but some dirty clothes and a few pairs of clean socks and underwear. "I don't think I have anything in here that is going to fit."

"Don't worry about it. I'll sleep in my clothes. But if you're okay with it, I may take off my pants. Cool?"

"You're wearing underwear, right?"

"Nope. Freeballing."

"Then keep the pants on. I don't want to wake up with something squishy pressed against me," she said.

"Something squishy, eh? I don't want to know what guys you have been sleeping with." There was an edge of jealousy in his voice.

"Oh, there was nothing soft going on with any of the men I've slept with." In truth, she'd only slept with one guy. That had been over a year ago, and their relationship had ended after she had caught him cheating. Since then, she'd sworn off sex, but now, within Jasper's reach, her celibacy seemed like a ridiculous idea.

"I don't know want to know." Jasper said, his playfulness gone. He walked over to the light switch by the door and clicked off the overhead light. "Get changed. I won't watch."

She took out a pair of her barely worn boxers and a dirty tank top. She slowly lifted off her dress, letting the cold air of the room rush against her skin, cooling the heat of her unwelcome desire. The red dress she had worn was the only sexy thing she owned, and she had wasted it on Devon.

Glancing back, Jasper had sat down on the other side of the bed, judiciously diverting his gaze. Disappointment crept through her. Unclasping the back of her bra, she slipped it from her shoulders and dropped it into the bag.

Her self-consciousness took over as she changed and quickly slipped between the cool sheets of the bed. How she wished she had something that resembled one of those scantily clad women in an underwear catalogue that men always drooled over. As it was, the only model she could have passed for was one out of a postdated Sears catalog.

She rolled on her side, afraid that if she faced him in the thin light of the bedside lamp, she wouldn't be able to control her need to feel him against her.

At least she wouldn't have to worry about him being so attracted to her that he couldn't help himself. Although, it would have been far better than okay if he let his warm fingers trail down her skin all the way to the soft mound of flesh between her thighs.

"Starling?"

"Hmm?" she asked, keeping her back to him as he perched on the side of the bed.

"I have to tell you something."

She rolled over. "What?"

"I … I was the one who was sent to keep your mother safe. We knew about the Catharterians and that there was a faction who might come after the two of you, but we didn't realize the full threat. I didn't take the warning seriously; I was still dealing with the fallout after the deaths in Montana. And … and … I'm sorry."

He rested his warm hand on her shoulder and softly stroked her bare skin. His eyes were filled with remorse. He clearly expected that she would be angry or hurt, but instead there was only the ache of pity. What a weight he must have carried to believe that he alone was responsible for her mother's death. "Jasper, there were so many things going on in my mother's life. She had made enemies."

"I should have been there to save her."

"I should have too, Jasper." She put her hand on his. Her entire body tingled.

"Can you forgive me?" Jasper's voice only made the tingle intensify.

"We both made a mistake," she said.

The bed bumped against the wall as he lay down next to her. "You're not afraid of the dark, are you?" he asked tenderly.

"I'm not afraid of the dark, only of the things in the night that I don't expect." Her cheeks warmed.

Jasper cleared his throat. "I'll do my best to keep anything *unexpected* at bay."

"You better, or remember those defensive maneuvers? Don't think I won't use them," she said lightly, as she frantically hoped he could read between the lines of her banter.

"Can you feel that?"

She went still, but felt nothing. "What?"

"That's me shaking with fear." He chuckled.

"Ah, I thought it was an earthquake."

"Oh, you think that was an earthquake … if given the chance, I could make your earth shatter."

She tried to not read too much into his words, but she didn't know exactly what to say. She wished she were one of those sex vixens from a Saturday night movie, a woman who had all the right moves and could make a man drop to his knees in a second. Starling paused. She was a sex vixen. When she had used her gift in the past, she had wrapped the boy around her finger. Maybe she could practice using her power on Jasper.

But the thought of treating Jasper like she planned on treating Devon bothered her. He deserved better. True seduction, seduction that meant something, needed control. And that level of seduction was best left to her nymph sisters who knew what in the hell they were doing. There had to be baby steps into the realm of sex vixen; her first was sharpening her flirtation skills. As it was, if she tried to seduce anyone, she'd probably only end up with another pizza.

"'Night, Starling." Jasper leaned away and clicked off the light. "If you need anything, let me know. I don't want you roaming around in the dark. I'd hate for you to find something unexpected."

"'Night, Jasper." A thin seam of light poured out from under the crack of the door, filling the room with deep shadows.

The minutes twisted by while she listened to the calm melody of his breathing. The sound was rhythmic and constant, the sounds of sleep. It was so quiet, it made the beautiful agony of not feeling his touch against her skin only the more painful. She stroked her arm, trying to remember exactly how good it had felt when he'd touched her last. He had to be fantastic in bed; she'd bet he was the kind of man who always made sure the woman was satisfied before thinking of himself.

Her entire body warmed and she rolled on her back. Lifting her shirt so her stomach lay bare, she continued tracing her fingers up and down her skin. The soft flesh of her belly was nothing like his muscular core.

If she ran her fingers over him, would he tense or relax under her touch?

Her hands moved down, over the cloth of her boxers, and she rubbed, soft and slow. She bit her lip as she tried to stop from moaning. She couldn't make any noise and give away what she was doing—she would never survive the embarrassment if he caught her. Her fingers swirled faster at the danger of being discovered.

Jasper shifted in the bed and she stopped. His breathing grew more rapid. "Don't stop," he whispered, his voice hoarse. "I don't want you to stop."

"What?" she asked, trying to sound innocent, but her breathlessness had to speak of her guilt.

Jasper reached over and put his hand atop hers. He started to swirl. It was impossible to stop the rich moan that escaped her throat. Even her toes tingled with the euphoria of his touch, but she didn't want to be alone in her ecstasy, so she slipped her fingers out from beneath his. Reaching over, she slid her hand under the elastic of his boxers. He was hot and rock hard as she worked his length.

"I thought we were going to be smart," she said, her tone heavy with lust.

"Smart be damned." Jasper leaned over, brushing his lips over her. His breath poured over her lips, making her taste his sweet desire.

"Oh my God," he said in almost a whimper. "Starling … "

She moved away from his fingers, pulled off her underwear with her free hand, and threw them on the floor. Moving between his thighs, she kissed the soft curves of the muscles on his stomach, inching down until she reached the hard arch of his hips. She eased down his underwear, revealing every inch of him in the faint light. Bruises lined his torso, and there was a scrape on his shoulder.

"Are you sure you are up to this?" She traced her finger lightly over a bruise that had risen near the top of right hip.

"Don't worry about me. I'm fine as long as I'm here with you."

She drew in a breath. He was even better than she had imagined.

"Come here," Jasper whispered, his voice soft and sexy. She moved on top of his muscular body. Reaching up, he lifted the edge of her tank top and drew it over her head. It met the heap of clothing on the floor.

"Here I thought you were a nice guy," she said with a sexy smile.

"I am nice." He reached up and cupped her breasts, running his callused thumb over her nub, making twinges of lust flash through her. "You know the best thing about nice guys?"

"Hmmm?"

"Nice guys always finish last." He smiled up at her, a diamond-like sparkle in his eyes. Sitting up, he licked the pink, erect tip of her nipple. He surrounded her flesh with his lips and gently sucked, driving pangs of want straight to the intersection of her thighs.

Dropping her head back, she moaned, deep and long, lavishing in the suction of his mouth.

Dipping her hips, she rolled her body against his; the action made his soft kiss harden. She leaned into his ear as she rocked her body over his. "I want you."

He answered with a sharp inhale, the cool air pulling over her hot, wet nipple.

He took hold of her panties and ripped the sides.

"That's not something a nice guy would do … " she said, breathlessly.

Her body ached with desire as he pulled the moist fabric from between her thighs.

He tossed her torn panties to the floor. "Too nice isn't what you want."

She chuckled, but the sound was cut off by him running his warm, moist kiss down the side of her neck. Breathing into his hair, she took in a long draw of his scent, hot and manly, the rich odors of lust and sweat.

"No, it's not." Reaching down, she took him in her hand and led him to her body's folds. Instead of being gentle, she drove him deep inside. His body tensed beneath her and he lifted his hips, sliding deeper.

Her body tingled as she rode him, faster and faster, dipping and twisting her hips in motion to the sounds of his breathing. Stars formed at the edges of her vision as a bubble of euphoria threatened to explode inside of her.

She slowed the movement of her hips, but as she did, he flipped her on her back. Her toes curled, and her fingers dug into his skin as he drove deep and broke the fragile bubble, throwing her into the throes of orgasmic pulsation.

There was something to be said for nice guys.

Chapter Seventeen

The bedroom door opened. "Get up," Devon ordered. His face was locked into a tight scowl as Jasper moved his arm from under Starling's head. She had fallen asleep on his bicep and he clenched his numb hand, trying to regain feeling. "We have to meet Virginia."

Devon glanced at Starling and his scowl deepened. "You have two minutes. Make yourselves presentable." He threw a clean set of black dress pants and a white, button-up shirt for Jasper and a white dress for Starling.

"Thanks," she said. Sitting up, she pulled up the sheet, covering her naked chest, and grabbed the dress from the end of the bed.

Devon grumbled under his breath. He slammed the door shut.

"Do you think he knows what we did?" Starling asked.

"I'm not sure if you are aware of this, but you are not what I would call quiet in the bedroom."

Starling's cheeks reddened. She pulled the white dress over her head, covering her face.

"Don't get me wrong, I'm not complaining," he said as he recalled the way her body pitched and writhed in the throes of her ecstasy. He hardened at the thought of her soft skin and her little, pink nipples.

He reached over and brushed a strand of wayward hair from her face. "When we get out of here, I fully intend on letting you be as loud as you want to be."

"Are you saying you want this to be more than a one night thing?"

"Don't you?"

"It's just not like you. The last time you and I spent time together, you left the next day."

"I did what I thought was right, Starling. You have to know that."

"All I know was that for the first time I really cared about someone, and then you left me."

"I couldn't stay, sweetheart. I had to go back to the Sisterhood and report what had happened. I had to protect you the only way I could—even if it meant leaving you behind."

"I get it, but please don't do that to me again, promise?"

He gave her a long look. The pain in her eyes made him want to promise he would never leave her alone. But right now, in the precarious situation in which they found themselves, making a promise like that would be easy—keeping it could prove to be impossible, since he was unlikely to make it out of these headquarters alive. Then again, she most likely needed some kind of reassurance, something that would let her know everything would be okay.

"I promise I'll try to stay with you, no matter what it takes."

She gave him a sideways glance, as if she knew how empty those words were.

There was a knock on the door. "Hurry up!" Devon yelled.

"What are we going to do about him?" Starling whispered.

"Are you still willing to seduce him? It may be our only chance to figure out what the hell is going on."

"You won't be jealous if I touch him?"

Just the thought made a fire roil up in his belly, but he tried to extinguish the feeling. "As long as you don't try any of your *defensive maneuvers* that you used on me, we should be okay," he said with a gentle wink.

Starling's laughter was brittle. "Don't worry. I only use those types of moves on the men I ... care about."

Jasper couldn't help but notice her long pause. Had she wanted to say love?

He should have never let things get as far as they had last night. He'd once again failed in keeping her safe—he had put her heart and life in danger.

Goddamn it.

"We need to go." He stood up and dressed quickly. "Devon is waiting. The sooner you deal with him, the faster we may get out of this hellhole."

She followed his lead, but her smile disappeared. "Jasper, you okay?"

"Yeah."

"Look, I don't have to seduce Devon if you don't want me to."

"What?" Jasper jerked. "No, seduce him. You need to. You *have* to."

"If you're going to be upset about it, we can find another way."

"I'm not upset because of Devon. I don't give a shit about that asshat."

"Then what's wrong?"

"Nothing. Let's go," Jasper said, trying not be too gruff. She couldn't worry about him. She needed to concentrate on getting out. "Just find out where you can get the books and then how you can get out of here."

"You mean how *we* can get out of here."

"Right." Jasper said, walking to the door and turning the handle. "We."

Starling stepped beside him and stopped. She laid her hand on his stubble-ridden cheek. "Don't forget that you made me a promise ... I expect you to keep it." She rose on her tiptoes and kissed him. He put his arm around her waist and put his other hand over hers on his cheek and then sank into the depths of her kiss.

She stepped back, out of his arms. "Let's go."

He pulled the door open. Devon waited for them in the hall.

"Here," Devon said, handing them both black cloaks. "Put these on." Devon slipped one over his clothes, tied a bow with the string under his chin, and drew the hood over his head. The hood dipped low, covering the man's eyes and nose so that only his mouth showed. Devon slipped it back slightly on his head so he could look at them. "Make sure to wear your hood."

He was trying to hide them once again. Jasper glanced at Starling and motioned toward Jasper, urging her to begin before someone had the chance to run interference. She nodded and stepped next to Devon.

"Where are you taking us?" she asked.

Devon sneered. "Wherever I want. Now shut up and put on your cloak."

Starling slipped on the hooded cloak. Holding the edges, she eyed Devon. "Can you help me?" she asked, her voice syrupy sweet.

He frowned. "Why don't you ask your lover? From what I heard, he seemed more than happy to give you a hand last night."

"I don't know what you're talking about, Devon," she said, repeating his name, this time her voice even sweeter. She laid her hand on the man's arm and stroked the black fabric of his cloak with her thumb.

"I know what you are doing, so you can stop," Devon grumbled. His face was harsh and cold. He drew back from her touch.

"What? I'm not doing anything. I just need a little help with my cloak. Please?" She lifted her chin, making room for Devon to tie her cloak's strings.

"You can't seduce me. I'm above that," Devon said. He took the ties under her neck and started to tie.

Jasper cringed at the sight of Devon's hands so close to Starling's exposed neck. One little move, one grab of the hair, and she would be gone. He inched closer, but stopped. He had to trust Starling and her ability. Even if that meant she was temporarily in harm's way.

Starling reached up and touched the bare skin of Devon's hand. "Thank you." A strange energy whipped through the air, lashing against Jasper like a wave, strong and weak in its ebb and flow. His mind turned fuzzy, and for a moment, he was back in her arms the night before, his tongue flicking over the hard nubs on the tips of her breasts, kissing her bare skin as he worked his way down her stomach toward her hidden pleasures.

No. No. He had to concentrate. She didn't love him. This energy wasn't for him. He had to keep his wits. He couldn't think about pressing his naked body against hers, or how warm she had felt against him, how wet …

He glanced over at Devon. The asshat's face was slack as he stared guppy-mouthed at Starling. Above seduction, his ass.

"Devon," Starling cooed, reaching up and running her fingers down the edge of their captor's right ear and tugging on his ear lobe. "How can we get out of here?"

"You don't want to leave me, do you?"

"No … But I need to know how to get out in case we are separated."

"All the exits are being watched by Virginia's men. You can't get out without me."

"Where are we going?"

"I can't tell you," he said, his voice as weak as his resolve.

Starling smiled. There was another wave of energy. This time the energy was steady, strong, and full of intention. Jasper slipped back into his thoughts of last night: her sitting on top of him, her long hair slipping down her shoulders, down her back as her hips rolled.

"Devon?" Starling's voice pulled Jasper out of his lustful stupor. "Where are you taking us, baby?" she asked.

Jealousy bubbled up in Jasper's core as she ran her hand down Devon's arm and slipped her fingers between the asshat's.

"We're going to sanctuary." Devon's voice trembled.

"What is happening there?"

"I don't know. Ms. Virginia wouldn't tell me."

"What do you know?" Starling touched Devon's cheek with her free hand.

"I just got off the phone with Harper," he said. "It looks like she'll be coming down—turns out she has agreed to trade." He gave Jasper a sickening sneer.

"Harper will be here? When?" Starling asked with a wheeze.

"We sent a man to the airport an hour ago. They should be arriving with the drugs anytime."

"With the drugs?" Starling paused. "The GX 149?"

"What else?" Devon shrugged. "She's agreed to exchange the rest of the drugs and the formula for your release."

"For *my* release? What about Jasper?"

"There aren't enough drugs in the world for Virginia to release him. She vowed that I would get my chance to kill him."

Starling glanced at him. Her eyes were wide. "You can't hurt him, Devon. Jasper is my bodyguard. You don't want to upset me, do you?"

Devon didn't answer. He blinked, almost as if he was trying to fight off Starling's energy.

She must have noticed because she let go of his hand. Leaning in, she grasped Devon's face with both of her hands and pressed her lips against his. Jasper tried to subdue his anger, but a grumble rolled through him.

Starling's face pinched as Devon's lips parted and his tongue moved over her bottom lip.

He couldn't handle it. He pushed Devon back, out of Starling's hands. "Back the fuck off."

"Jasper! Stop!" Starling moved after Devon.

Guilt poured through him, dousing his rage. Why couldn't he control himself? He was better than this. He *had* to be better than this. "I'm sorry, Starling."

Devon looked dazedly out at Starling. "Are you okay, little bird?" he asked sweetly, still entranced.

Jasper exhaled with relief. "I'll stop, Starling, but please don't kiss him again in front of me. I know I agreed to you seducing him, but I can't handle seeing it. I think your spell is rubbing off on me. I can't control my anger."

"Huh?" Devon looked over at him like he was a stranger moving in on his girlfriend. "Who are you?"

"What did you do to him?" Jasper addressed Starling. "He's even dumber than usual."

Devon looked at him, doe-eyed. "I take offense to that, man."

"See what I mean?"

"Did he do something to hurt you, little bird?" Devon said, glancing over at him. "Do you want me to kill him?"

"Devon, who will be in the sanctuary?" he asked.

"What's sanctuary?"

Starling stared at the stunned lump. "The kiss was too much."

"Ya think?" Jasper shook his head. "You are going to need a little more practice with your *feminine wiles*."

"Okay, old man."

"As long as I'm *your* old man."

"Of course." She smiled. "In the meantime, what are we going to do with fish-mouth?" she asked, motioning at the slack-jawed Devon, who was staring blankly at her face.

"He isn't going to be of any use to us unless you can take back some of your energy."

"I barely know how to send out the energy. I don't think I can get it back. It's not like a boomerang."

Jasper laughed as he opened the door to their room. "Then he is no good to us." He pointed toward the bed covered in the love-wrinkled sheets.

"Devon, baby?" she asked in a mesmerizing tone.

"Huh?" He blinked as he stared at her. "Yes, little bird?"

"Can you stay here?"

The man nodded like an obedient love slave.

"Don't leave and don't tell anyone where we have gone. Okay?"

"Okay, my little bird." Devon walked into the room and sat down on the edge of the bed. "I'll stay here forever as long as you come back for me. Promise."

"We'll see, baby. Be a good boy." Starling closed the door. "Now what are we going to do? I have no idea where to find the sanctuary."

Jasper tugged on the hood of the cloak. "The good news is that now we have a way to move around without drawing too much attention."

"We need to find Harper," Starling said.

"If we get lucky, she'll be in the sanctuary like she's supposed to be."

"Harper would never walk into this place without a plan. She'd never put us all in danger if she didn't have something up her sleeve, especially if my dad knows what's going on."

"Who would she be working with?"

"Since you're already here ... that only leaves the Sisterhood."

Chapter Eighteen

They backtracked through headquarters until Starling caught the rich scent of cooking meats and rice that wafted from the dining hall. She tried to recall the exact route she had taken from the elevators, but after so many rights and lefts, it was hard to remember exactly what direction she had come from. Before she could start formulating their escape, she needed to find Harper.

Virginia had the upper hand. After erasing Edward's soul, it wasn't hard to imagine all the vile things Virginia would be willing to do to get what the Catharterians wanted from Harper.

"Do you think she's okay?" Starling whispered.

"Harper?"

"No, Virginia," she scoffed with a nervous laugh.

"Harper's fine. Knowing her, she's probably got Chance at her side."

"Do you think they'd let Chance in?"

"I doubt she would let them bring her down here without some kind of bodyguard." He looked away, but not before she caught a glimpse of the worry in his eyes. The speed of his footsteps increased.

She hurried to stay beside him. "What do you think they would do to us if they find out that we are running around headquarters, or they find Devon in our room?"

"I think it's better if we don't find out."

She tried to shrug off the feeling of malevolence that spread through her as they made their way into the dining hall.

Sitting at the far table was a group of men and women, making Starling forget about her dreams of food. The group of people looked up at them.

"What are you doing?" a man with a southern accent asked as he stood up.

Starling stopped and started to turn on her heel. They shouldn't have come this way. They should have kept to the shadows and avoided anywhere they could run into the shifters. Her body tingled with fear.

Jasper laid his hand on the small of her back. "Just stay quiet," he whispered, with a reassuring pat. "We'll get out of this."

The vulture man walked toward them. "Hear me? What're y'all doing?"

Starling tensed, ready for a fight.

"We were just on the way to sanctuary. Got a little lost."

"I'd say. And you guys are late. They started twenty minutes ago," the man said. "Where y'all from?" he asked as he led them out of the dining hall through a far door.

"Idaho," Jasper said.

"That's great. Glad y'all could make it down for the meeting. This is a big one—could change it all." The man glanced over at her. "Which way you gonna vote?"

What could she possibly say that wouldn't draw the man's suspicion? She swallowed back the lump in her throat. "There's only one vote, am I right?" She gave a nervous laugh.

"Right. Right." The man nodded. "That Virginia is a crazy bitch. We can't let her get what she wants from the council."

"You got that right," Jasper said. "You have any idea how the voting is going to play out?"

The man walked them down a hall. "It's hard to say." He shrugged. "Right now she has a lot of support from the local group. They want blood for everything that has happened with the nymphs. But for the rest of us … well, you know."

No, she didn't, but now was hardly the time to ask. "The nymphs aren't to blame. It was Dr. Redbird who started that war."

The shifter turned and looked at her with a raised brow. "I agree. Virginia's sister was just as crazy, but this war has been a long time coming. The old nymph president had given her word to work with us. I don't care if they overthrew their president—they should follow through on their agreements."

What was he talking about? Was all this the former leader of the Sisterhood, Katarina's, fault? Had Katarina made some kind of deal with the vultures? What other deals had she made? More than that, if Kat had made a deal, it meant Ariadne must have known, or at the very least she must have found out. Why hadn't she told the Sisterhood? Or why had the Sisterhood left the rest of the nymphs in the dark?

"I agree. Deals are important, but Dr. Redbird took it too far," Jasper said, running his fingers over the bruise under his eye.

"There's no question about that, but you know her—act first, think later." He stopped outside of a large black door. "She's just like her sister. If it hadn't been for Virginia, we would have never had the problems we do now. It's just a damn fine thing that we have President Kitchings—without him we would have never gotten our hands on the bank. We would still be struggling to meet our financial needs."

"Absolutely," Starling said. So this was the story behind those hundreds of websites she found in her search for the lockbox that had cited the former bank with fraud. "The vultures had something to do with the bank's takedown?" As soon as the words fell from her lips, Jasper cringed.

"What?" the man said, a shocked look on his face. "We took a vote five years ago. We set them up to take a fall. Don't you remember?"

"I'm sure you remember, don't you?" Jasper gripped her shoulder like she was a good friend … who had made a fatal mistake.

"I'm such a moron sometimes. I just forgot!" Starling replied, her tone two octaves too high. She gave another nervous laugh. It was a good thing she never wanted to be a professional gambler; cool and collected would never be her strong suit.

The man stared at her like he was trying to read her mind. "The sanctuary is that way," he said, pointing vaguely down the hall.

If the group had the power to take down a national bank, it was hard to think of a way she and Jasper could make it out of their headquarters. She could feel the possibility of survival slipping out of her grasp.

Jasper stepped forward and put his hand on the doorknob. "Thanks for showing us the way to the sanctuary. Appreciate your help."

"Mmm hmm," the man replied as he continued to stare. He glanced over at Jasper. "Why don't I walk you in? Hate for you two to get lost again."

The way he talked made her skin prickle with nervousness. She slipped out of Jasper's grasp.

"We'll be fine, really." She stepped next to the man and put her hand over his. "We have everything under control." The energy seeped out of her, the warmth reminding her of the way it felt to shift into her swan form, but different, more intense. "Why don't you stay here, make sure no one comes or goes from the room?" She reached up with her other hand and ran her finger over the weak line of his jaw.

His eyes widened as her spell took effect. "What's your name?" he asked, his voice low and sultry.

"Don't worry, sweetheart. Just remember that you must protect me and my friend. No matter what you hear, do not enter the room. Just wait for us to return. Understand?"

"Yes, ma'am." The man leaned in, taking in a long inhale. "You smell like magnolias. I love magnolias."

She sniffed but smelled nothing but the dank, earthy scent of the underground lair. "Watch the doors."

She glanced over at Jasper. His eyes had widened, but it wasn't like the last time she'd used her gift with Devon. This time, Jasper's mouth hadn't grown slack. Perhaps he was more immune to her charms or, just maybe, she had gotten more control over her ability for seduction. She hoped for the latter.

The man walked over to a keypad on the wall by the doors and entered a few numbers. The door buzzed. "Here, let me get that for you," he said, stepping between Starling and Jasper as if he didn't even realize there was another person in the hall.

The door squeaked as he pulled it open, exposing a long, entrance hall that looked eerily similar to the one she had snuck into from the mausoleum. There was row after row of pictures of former presidents and vice presidents, but nothing else to give away the significance of the place.

She walked through the entrance, Jasper close at her heels. On their left were three doors identical to the ones on their right. "What do you think is in here?"

"I don't know, but this place is a helluva lot bigger than what I thought. There could be thousands of Catharterians."

"At least we know Walter and his men have left."

"But there could be many more. I underestimated their power."

The ball in her stomach tightened as he voiced her fear. "Devon made it sound like it was only going to be Virginia and Harper. Let's hope they are the only ones here."

"Sure, but the people in the dining hall hinted this was a huge meeting of superiors. Do you think Virginia was going to tell them about us?"

"I have no idea, but we better get to Harper before they figure out she doesn't have any more GX 149 to offer—otherwise there are going to be three of us who don't make it out of here."

They moved down the hall as Starling listened for any sound. Nearing the middle door on their right, she was met by the quiet murmur of women talking. "There's really no need," Virginia's rasping voice echoed out into the corridor. "Devon will be along any time. What harm can a barely legal nymph and her Neanderthal of a bodyguard do?"

"You're right, Ms. Virginia," a man answered.

"I've heard that voice," Jasper whispered. "It's the man who took me hostage. The old guy."

"Do you think we should go back and search for the president? Maybe the guy outside the doors could tell him where we could find him?"

"Why would we do that?"

"If Virginia is keeping secrets from him, maybe we can use her sedition to our advantage."

"I think we're damned if we do and damned if we don't. There's no telling what the president will do to us if he finds out we are here—Virginia might be the weaker link, as hard as that is to believe. If we can just take her and her goon squad down, we might have a chance."

"That doesn't move us any closer to finding the books, Jasper."

"Right … the damned books."

"They're not just some *damned* books. Those books are the only chance I have not to lose my mind as soon as we get out of here. Without them I'll never be able to get a handle on the spirits—and what happens if you or someone else I lo—" She stopped mid-word. "I mean, *care* about, is possessed? I can't go through that again."

His eyes softened as he gazed at her. The oasis of blue had disappeared, leaving only a glimpse of light in the darkness of his eyes. "Starling, what if we don't get those books?"

"Then I'm as good as dead—either I will go crazy or one of the spirits will take me down. Asclepius made it more than clear that they wouldn't leave me alone until I got the books—I think they need them as badly as I do. If I go above without them, it is hard to tell what they will do to me."

Jasper wrapped his arm around her and nuzzled her hair. He took in a long breath. Being that close to him made tears well in her eyes. So many things could go wrong. This could be the last time they would have the chance to be together. And even if they made it out of here, they could never be together, thanks to her curse. She sank into his arms, letting the heat of his touch melt into a memory.

"Don't worry, sweetheart. I will get the books for you. No matter what it takes. But first we need to find out if Harper is in there or if Devon was only bluffing."

The voices on the other side of the door grew louder and the door handle shifted. Starling started to move toward the door, but Jasper held on, stopping her from advancing. "This way," he said, pointing in the opposite direction down the hall.

She took a step toward Jasper as the door opened. He pushed her behind him, shielding her from whatever or whoever was behind the door.

"Just keep Kitchings away from here. Got it?" Virginia's shrill voice pitched into the hall.

"No prob—" the man paused. "What in the holy hell?"

Starling stepped out from behind Jasper to see a bald old man, his eyes squinted and his nostrils flared with rage.

"What is it, Jim?"

"Our guests are here, without their keeper."

"What?" Virginia stepped out into the hallway and she stared at them. "Where's Devon?"

The man's lips pulled back into a sneering smile. "Y'all didn't touch our boy, did ya?"

"Not at all. I think he was just getting tired of your company," Starling said.

"Shut up. Where's Devon?" Virginia repeated the man's question.

"I have no idea," Jasper answered.

"I told you we couldn't trust him. He only wanted in that lil tramp's pants. He never really believed in the cause," Jim grumbled.

"Shut up, Jim. Devon would never turn against us."

"Walter did. What if he's with Kitchings now? What if he's tellin' him all about our plan?"

"I said *shut up*, Jim." Virginia turned toward him, her lips turned up like a growling dog. "Walter is gone. He told me he was leaving."

"Is Harper here?" Starling asked, trying not to let the rising tide of fear crash over into her voice.

Virginia's eyes narrowed into tight slits. "She will be arriving any minute. There was a slight hiccup in her arrival."

"Is she okay?" Starling pressed.

"If I were you," Virginia said, her tone low and menacing, "I would be more worried about myself."

"Well, that is the difference between you and me, Virginia," she said, summoning every ounce of her courage. "I care more about others than about myself."

"That's fine, but that stupidity is very close to getting you killed."

A wiggle of hope stole through Starling. Maybe Harper had done the right thing and not allowed herself to be put in danger with the Catharterians—or better yet, maybe she had started taking them down. Starling smiled as she thought of Harper breaking into headquarters, guns ablaze.

Chapter Nineteen

Inadequate wasn't just a state of being. No, for Jasper it was all encompassing. He had never felt so helpless, but then again he'd never been held hostage in an underground headquarters. At least he could take a small amount of comfort in the fact that Virginia had chosen not to tie him to a chair as Jim had done.

Yet, there was little comfort in the cardboard box-sized room. He, Virginia, and Starling could barely squeeze around the desk without each of them touching elbows.

"This is one hell of a sanctuary," he grumbled.

"This isn't the sanctuary," Virginia said. "This is my office."

"You've got to be kidding me. They have one empty room after another, but they find the smallest of all of them and give it to you? Either you are a college professor or someone out there hates you."

Virginia answered him with a glare. Opening a drawer, she pulled out a black cloak that matched his and Starling's. "As soon as Jim gets back with Devon, I will join the rest of the council—they are already having their meeting. If everything goes according to plan, they will see the value in my proposal. From there, we will swing the vote my way and then begin the fertility treatments."

"Does that mean you will let us go?" Starling asked.

"I told you," Virginia closed the desk's drawer. "I need proof that it works. Until then, you will have to stay with us. If the drugs you give us fail, then we will have to take other, more invasive measures to study what in your chemistry allows the drugs to work."

"That won't happen." Jasper slammed his fist down on Virginia's desk. "Once you get the drugs from Harper you have to let us go."

"I don't *have* to do anything. Did you forget that you are a prisoner here? You have no rights … not even to live. In fact, you're lucky that I have allowed you to live this long, Jasper."

Some of his anger seeped out. She was right. Why had they let him live so long?

"You need me," he countered.

Virginia laughed. "Why would we need some worthless bodyguard?"

"He's not worthless," Starling said with a jerk.

"Really? He's failed to save you every time you needed him. In fact, even now, he's done nothing to help you." Virginia dropped the cloak into her lap. "If we had bodyguards as bad as yours, we'd all be dead."

His laughter exploded deep from his core. "No matter how *good* your bodyguards are, they won't be able keep you alive. After we get out of here, I will make sure that you die."

"Then I have nothing to worry about."

The door to the office flew open. "What in the hell are you doing, Virginia?" A man burst in, his black cloak pulled tightly over his stout belly. His face was long and round and pulled into an angry pucker. "I told you to stay the hell out of this mess."

The man stopped and stared at Jasper and Starling. "You have got to be kidding me. I thought Devon had just gone off his rocker."

"What happened to Devon?" Virginia blanched.

"Our guards found him walking down the dorm hall. He was acting crazy; talking nonsense about a nymph and her bodyguard being inside the walls of headquarters. He even hit one of the guards when they tried to restrain him. Kept repeating how he was looking for *his* nymph."

Virginia glanced over at Starling.

"It wasn't hard to connect the dots, Virginia." The man seethed. "I told you not to do anything stupid. Yet, here we are.

Once again." He stared at Starling as he took deep, long breaths followed with even longer exhales as he tried to calm his temper. "Now, I can assume that as this woman isn't one of us, she must be the nymph, Starling, that Devon was talking about."

Virginia jumped to her feet. "Steve, it's not what you think. Really."

"How is this not what I think it is? I told you to stay the fuck away from the nymphs. I told you we would find another way. But no, you and your shoot-now-ask-questions-later attitude is the reason that I'm voting to have you removed from your role as vice president."

"Steve, you don't understand … "

"Don't call me Steve. I'm the president. You lost any right to call me Steve when I moved out of our marital bed. Did you really think you could get me back by going rogue? We had a strategy. The council voted on a strategy."

"Just give me a chance."

"Your chances disappeared when you went against us … Damn it, you went against *me*."

Virginia's face turned from white to a pale green. "President Kitchings, I wanted to bring it up to the council at today's meeting. I have a plan. You just need to listen."

"Shut your mouth. You are nothing but a pain in my ass. Put on your cloak. I will meet you and your friends," he said, motioning toward Jasper and Starling, "in the sanctuary. You have two minutes. If you're late, I will have you *taken care of*."

"You wouldn't go against the council. You need a full vote to strip me of my position … or my life."

"You needed voter support, too, but no … you took action without it. Once the council knows what you've done, I don't think they'll have a problem with me hastening your end. Now get your ass to the sanctuary if you even want a chance to plead your case."

"You make it sound like I don't have much of a case to plead." Virginia eyed the door like a trapped animal looking for escape.

"We all want the same thing—at least I thought we did," President Kitchings answered.

"We do," Virginia supplicated.

"Then you better be ready to prove it." The president walked out.

Jasper loved watching Virginia being stricken from her pedestal.

Virginia glared at Starling. "What did you do to Devon?"

"Nothing you wouldn't have done," Starling replied. Her shoulders had lightened and some of the color had returned to her face. The president's words must have lifted some of her fear.

"Such a bitch." Virginia turned to Jasper. Her eyes had grown darker. "You will never make it out of here alive. Regardless of what happens to me."

"At least if I go down, I know you are going to go down with me." Jasper stood up and moved toward the door, Starling close at his heels.

"What in the hell do you think you're doing?" Virginia growled.

"We're going to the sanctuary. You don't have power over us now that the president knows we're here."

Virginia slid open the top drawer of her desk and pulled out a 9mm. The black handgun fit in her hand like it was made for her and her murderous grip. "You will not go against me."

He pushed Starling behind him. "You are wrong about so many things."

"No, I'm not!" Virginia cried, dropping her finger from the side of the gun to the trigger. "You don't know anything. I'm going to get my army. We are going to take down Zeus!"

"You want to take down a god?" Starling peeked around from behind him. "That's what this is all about? What in the hell does fertility have to do with taking down Zeus?"

"You're not the only set of supernaturals he cursed." The gun trembled in her hand.

"How did he curse you?" Starling rested her hand on his shoulder. She probably wanted him to move, but he refused to budge. Virginia held the gun. She could fire at any time. Starling wouldn't die from a bullet, but he couldn't let her be hurt like that. Not now. Not ever.

"You may not be able to fall in love with a man, but our curse is so much worse. We can never have children. Our demigod line is coming to an end. Soon there will be none of us left. And that's exactly what Zeus wants. He only wants a select few of his favored demigods to survive. He doesn't want us, the scavengers of death, to have a place at the table. He hated our Titan grandmother, Gaea, and our mother, Alecto, a fury. Zeus believes we're evil like others of our lineage. But we aren't devoted to the wicked—only death. We need death to live."

"How is feeding off death not something wicked?"

"How is seduction not wicked?" Virginia countered. "Look, we're not killing anyone—usually." She lowered the weapon slightly. "We just need the souls to power our bodies. That is why we live here," she said motioning upward, "under the graveyard. We need the dead's energy to live."

"And the drugs."

"Yes, if we get the GX 149 we can strengthen our numbers. Maybe one day we can grow large enough to mount a force against Zeus. Maybe we can get him to lift his curse."

"Why didn't you and your council just go to the Sisterhood to gain access to the drugs?" Starling countered.

"Really? You don't think we've already done that?"

"When?" Jasper stared at the gun in Virginia's hand. Even though she had lowered the piece, they weren't out of danger.

"We met with Kat a few years back, when we first learned about the drugs. She made it abundantly clear that you and your kind would do nothing to help us. She treated us with nothing but hatred and derision—like we were trash just because of our penchant for death, like we were some kind of untouchables."

"Have you met with Ariadne?" Starling asked.

"She and her crew killed one of us before those meetings could take place. You and your kind," she said, glaring at Starling, the gun trembling higher, "started this war."

Jasper stepped forward and gently laid his hand on the gun, pressing it downward. "Virginia, we can figure this out. We can work out something where both groups get what they need. But you can't keep flagging us with that gun. Let me have it." He stared into her eyes; in the shadows of the room they looked almost completely black.

She let him pull the gun free of her hand. Jasper took the gun and slipped it in the back of his waistband and away from Virginia.

"I didn't start this," she pleaded. "I just want to have a baby. I promised my sister. We were going to do this together. And then … and then you killed her." Tears welled in her eyes as she looked at him. "You … *you* are the reason you're here. You deserve to die."

"She attacked a nymph. I was only doing my job. Dr. Redbird would have killed Harper." He stepped between Starling and Virginia.

She shot a look of hatred at Starling. "I know you would be willing to kill to get something you wanted. So was my sister. And so am I." Virginia lunged toward Starling, reaching for her hair.

Jasper jumped after her, grabbing her by the back of her cloak before she could reach Starling's sacred locks. He threw her to the concrete floor at Starling's feet. "You. Will. Not. Touch. Her," he said between breaths.

A speckle of blood dotted Virginia's lip as she glared at him with a look of hatred and disgust. "I just want to have a baby …"

Jasper grabbed her by her wrists and lifted her back up to her feet. "Let's go. Let's talk to the council. Maybe we can make someone see some sense. We don't have to continue like this, killing each other over old blood."

"It's only old because it wasn't someone you loved. You'd feel differently if it was her," Virginia said, with a soft sob as she motioned toward Starling with her chin. "But you ... you killed my sister."

"And your sister killed my mother." Starling gave him a pitying look, probably her way of trying to absolve him of any of residual guilt.

"I ... " He opened his mouth to speak, but he didn't know what to say. "Let's go, Virginia." He pushed her forward, past Starling.

"Should we really do this?" Starling asked.

"What else are we going to do, sweetheart?" He paused mid-stride. "I don't have a clue how to get out of here, and they already know we're here. I think our best bet is to go in there, make a case for trade, and get the hell out of here."

"It seems too easy," she said.

The knot in his stomach told him what she said was probably right. It was too easy. Something about it seemed off. The council must have had some kind of role in Virginia's plan—if nothing else, they turned a blind eye to some of her behavior. She had perpetuated an attack on a nymph in Crete.

"Virginia, you need to tell me the truth," Jasper said, still clenching her hands behind her back. "The council must have known what you were planning. Why didn't they stop you sooner?"

"They want the drugs, too; they just didn't want me to bring you or the nymph here." Virginia tried to pull her hands from his grip, forcing him to hold strong. "They had been working with Walter. He had a man tracking Starling, and when we found out she was coming here, we took a vote. The council decided against making a move and getting their hands dirty. They didn't want to escalate the conflict with the nymphs. Obviously, I didn't want to bring you into the headquarters either, but then Little Miss Snoop was in that mausoleum. Why do you think I let her listen in on us taking the White? It was too easy, laying a trap for her."

Starling drew her face menacingly close to Virginia's. "Where is it? Where are the books?" she asked in a dangerous voice.

"Get me out of here. Then make sure Harper gives me all the drugs and the formula. If you do that, I can convince Steve … er, President Kitchings that he and I can get pregnant. And maybe he will take me back." Virginia stared off into space. "He and I can rule indefinitely and our lineage will take over the council when they come of age."

"What happens if we go around you?" Starling challenged.

"I don't know, but it probably won't end with you both alive."

"I doubt that our chances of staying alive are any better staying with you. Why would I give you anything—all you've done is threaten Jasper. In case you missed it, I lo—" She stopped mid-word. "I *care* about him. And no one threatens the man I care about."

Jasper's heart stopped in his chest as she said the words. She had to know that to love him was dangerous. Her love was cursed—it would only end in his death. He would gladly die to be loved by her, without question. But he couldn't accept the heartbreak it would cause her.

"Let's go, Starling. We can't trust Virginia. She'll say anything she can to get out of this mess." He opened the door and led Virginia into the hall.

Voices bubbled out from underneath a set of double wooden doors at the end of the corridor. "Is that the sanctuary?" he asked, motioning toward the door.

Virginia's gaze remained pinned to the floor.

"I'll take that as a yes." Jasper pushed her down the hall.

"Are you sure, Jasper?" Starling looked at him with panic.

"It's okay, Starling. I will protect you. And there's only one thing I'm sure of—Virginia's word isn't worth the air it takes to speak it."

Some of the panic disappeared from her eyes. "If you think this is the right move, I've got your back. And no matter what happens, I know you did this for the right reasons."

"I … " He wanted to tell her that he loved her, that he wanted to hold her in his arms forever, but it he couldn't make himself say the words. He had to protect her.

"I know," Starling said, her voice quiet.

"Oh my God," Virginia grumbled. "Are you serious? Why don't you just fuck and get it over with?"

His cheeks burned.

Virginia laughed as she looked at him. "You already did … And you still can't tell her that you love her?" She motioned to Starling. "He says I'm not the one to be trusted, but come on. He's the one who is pathetic."

"Shut up, Virginia." She strode toward the sanctuary and threw open the doors.

Standing in the middle of the room, her arms behind her back, was Harper.

Blood dripped from Harper's chin, but she smiled and her face brightened as she saw them. "I thought you guys were dead."

President Kitchings walked toward them. "So glad you could join us. You're just in time to see your little friend die." He stepped beside Harper and raised a knife to her throat.

The man's words echoed through Jasper, drawing on his memories of Dr. Redbird and the night he'd killed her when protecting Starling. He shouldn't have quit killing there. He should have wiped out this entire species of death mongers.

Chapter Twenty

Starling's hands slipped from the door handle as she stared at the room full of black-cloaked vultures. Some of the birds were seated around a long, rectangular table in the center of the room, while others were gathered in small groups. All their eyes were on her.

"She's come," one of the vultures whispered to another.

She looked away from the mass of black birds to Harper, who had tears in her eyes. What had the vultures done?

"Are you okay?" Starling asked, moving past the table.

"Stop right there, girl," the president ordered.

Starling froze as the president's furious gaze pinned her.

"You should have left, Starling. You shouldn't still be here." The tears streamed down Harper's face, mixing with the blood on her chin, and dripped to the floor. "You have to let her go. She doesn't have anything you want." Harper tried to struggle, but Kitchings stopped her with a push of his blade. "You made me a deal."

"Be quiet, Harper." The president's silver knife cut into Harper's throat and dark red blood dotted the edge of the blade.

Jasper shoved Virginia in the room, making her sit in a chair at the table. A bird was etched in the black surface, matching the one Starling had seen in the mausoleum.

"You kill her, I kill Virginia." He reached behind him and pulled the gun from his waistband. "You should have heard her in there, talking to us. She told us all about her scheme and your involvement."

Starling stepped beside him, following his lead.

"Virginia … " A flicker of pain moved through the president's face, but he quickly took control over his tell. "Put down the gun, Jasper. And let go of Virginia."

"Only if you let Harper go. Do we have a deal?"

President Kitchings moved the knife back from Harper's throat, leaving behind a thin bead of blood. "Let her go."

Jasper let go of Virginia's hands. "It doesn't have to be like this. We just want to negotiate."

"Negotiate?" President Kitchings glanced around the roomful of council members. Most of the group nodded, but a few shook their heads in refusal. After a long moment, he turned back to Jasper. "Put down your gun. There," he ordered, pointing toward the middle of the table, near the feet of the vulture carving.

"Harper, get behind me," Jasper said, motioning for her to stand beside Starling.

"You guys should have left," Harper said in a whisper. "I had everything under control."

Starling pointed at the thin line of blood on Harper's throat. "Looks like it."

"Okay, so not everything was going to plan," she murmured.

"Gun. Now." President Kitchings motioned for one of his guards. Moving forward, the man grabbed Virginia by the arm, led her to a chair behind the president, and sat her down.

"I want us all to get along here. No need for anyone else to get hurt." Jasper raised the gun above his head as he moved through the crowd. Starling rested her hand on his back as she followed him. His body radiated nervous heat and sweat built under her touch, but she couldn't be sure if it was him, her, or the combination of both their fear.

He stopped at the designated spot and sat the gun down on the end of the table. This vulture had the same crimson-red color as the bird in the mausoleum, the eye that had been an elevator button. Was it possible this table was an elevator as well?

Just to the right of the carving was a thin seam. To the left of Jasper's gun and the carving's feet was another.

Some of her fear dissipated. There was a way out. Maybe.

"Shall we sit?" the president motioned to the seats. "Let us start again." He walked to the head of the table, his bodyguards flanking him, and sat down. His men stayed standing at each of his sides.

She, Harper, and Jasper moved to the front of the table where the president motioned. Starling couldn't take her eyes off the gun they were leaving farther behind with every step. No one got near it as they all made their way to the seats around the rectangle.

"Now, I want to extend to you my sincerest apologies about my wife's behavior." He looked to his right where Virginia sat. "She has a habit of interfering—even after there has been a vote." He eyed her dangerously. "I assure you that she will be dealt with accordingly. And so will Harper for infiltrating our den."

"I was told to come here. I infiltrated nothing!" Harper challenged.

"Be that as it may, the council and I were not expecting a nymph to walk into our chambers spewing hatred."

"Your wife is threatening my step-daughter. My *spewing hatred* is the least of what I plan to do to Virginia," Harper spat.

Jasper leaned toward her in his chair. "Stop," he warned.

Harper glared at him. "Fine, you handle this." After a moment she leaned back in her chair, arms crossed over her chest.

Jasper nodded and turned back to the president. "President Kitchings, we—"

"We offer no apologies," Starling interrupted. "We did exactly what we needed to do. Your people have done nothing but try to steal my things, kidnap me, and hurt me since I arrived in Savannah."

Jasper's mouth was still open and his eyes were wide with surprise at her taking the lead. She laid her hand on his, in an attempt to reassure him that she didn't need him to do her dirty work.

"I know the Catharterians broke into Jenna's safe deposit and stole the *Libros Umbrarum*. Those were intended for me."

The president shifted in his seat. "I will not give you—"

"Stop." Starling raised her hand, putting a halt to the president's possible refusal. "After all I've been through to get the books, you are going to give me all three. Without the books, there's no way you will be getting the GX 149 or its formula."

The president laughed. "We had to take down a bank to get those books. Do you really think we are going to give them to you just so we can get some silly drugs? Drugs that we already have?" He pointed to a woman sitting three chairs down, on his right. She reached into a bag at her side and pulled out a familiar orange bottle.

"You and I both know that there aren't enough pills in there for your kind to get what they need."

"But there are enough pills to study and find out what makes them effective in fertility," the president challenged.

"And that could take years of research," Harper retorted.

"Do you have years to waste on research?" Starling continued. "We have the formula. But first, I need the books."

"We're aware. But you aren't getting those books." The president's face tightened as he tried to handle his emotions. He glared at Harper. "And it just so happens that you, Harper, and your friends are prisoners—and if you want everyone to make it out of this room alive, you will do as we wish." He sat forward as he tried to control the situation. "If you're smart, which I think you must be, you will take one of my teams back to your lab and we can keep you under watch while you make us a supply large enough to help with our population issues."

"And then what?" Harper retorted. "Then you will let us go? I doubt it."

"Why would we need to continue a relationship once we get our drugs?"

"Because your women will still be unable to become pregnant," Harper said.

"What are you talking about? We are demigods just like you. And if they work for your kind, why wouldn't they work for us?"

"Give Starling what she wants, and then I will give you the formula and our secret. Agreed?" Harper asked.

The president put his elbows on the table and tented his fingers in front of his face. "How do we know that we need something else besides the pills?"

"Hasn't it occurred to you that Carey, Starling's mother, had been taking the drugs for almost twenty years? She had one pregnancy. Now I'm sure she had more partners than just one in those years. Yet she never had another pregnancy." Harper paused for a moment.

"Starling, had your mother seen other men?" the president asked.

"She had boyfriends on and off when I was growing up." Starling cringed as she realized that her mother's sex life was being called into question.

"Do you think she had relations with these men?"

"She probably did. I didn't try to keep tabs on my mother's sex life."

"Right, right." President Kitchings laughed. "Did she ever have another pregnancy?"

"Not that I know of," Starling said.

"Do you know why that was?"

Starling shook her head. She'd never given thought to why she didn't have siblings. She'd always assumed it was because Mom hadn't wanted another child, not that there had been some secret to why she'd been an only child.

Harper patted her arm. "There were other nymphs who were taking the same medication; however, most never got pregnant. I'm more than happy to show you the number of women who successfully mated." She raised two fingers.

"I get your point, but we can't make a deal if we lose access to the *Libros.*" The president paused. "We need them. It's how we've gotten control over the souls like Edward and Molly who work for us. If we lose those books, we will likely have an army of ghosts after us."

"I know the feeling," Starling retorted.

They were at an impasse. They could not live without the books, but neither could she.

"There has to be a way we can come to an agreement."

"Instead of fighting, maybe we could become allies." President Kitchings tapped his fingers against his chin as he thought. "We could give you the books if we have continued access to their contents. In return for this, you give us the drugs, formula, and secret. In addition, you all can walk out of here with the knowledge that the war is over."

"What about Virginia and her men? They must be punished. Strip them of their feathers," Starling urged.

"I know you are angry, but she is still my wife. She has done wrong. She kidnapped you and your friend and in doing so, went against the council. In the process of her mutiny, she also committed a mortal sin of erasing a soul. If other supernatural beings hear of what she has done, it will our be our asses on the line." Kitchings shook his head in disgust. "She will be dealt with, but stripping her of her feathers is too harsh a punishment for her crime. She will lose everything."

"She deserves to be punished," Starling urged.

"You have to let them handle this, Starling," Jasper whispered. "We will have to forgive them for what they have done so we can make this deal."

Could she forgive them in order to make peace? If Jasper could move past Edward's possession, she could move past her kidnapping, but there was still the issue of her mother's death.

Her mother used to smile and wrap her arms around her when she had a tough day. Without a doubt her mother would have done that to her today. For once, Starling wished she could talk to the spirits down here. She would love to ask her mother what to do, whether it was okay to forgive the group for her death. But Starling did know where her responsibilities lay for a friend. "You have to free Molly B. from the mausoleum and let her safely cross to the other side. In exchange, you will give us the books and this war between us will be over."

"Done, so long as we come to an adequate agreement about the production of the GX 149," President Kitchings replied.

"What do you think, Harper?"

Harper nodded. "I already built my lab in Vegas. It's a few months away from opening it doors, but if they pay me cost plus twenty percent, I could turn the lab into a legitimate drug manufacturing plant within the year. Chance could finish his agreement with the casino and all of us could be set, at least financially, for life. As long as they are willing to sign an official agreement for peace and trade, I'm good."

"You can forgive the fact that these vultures tried to kill you? That they killed my mother?"

"As far as I can tell, Starling," Jasper said, "it wasn't *they* who killed your mother. It was Dr. Redbird, her sister, and their lackeys who put that together. Not the main council. Dr. Redbird is no longer an issue."

"We need to put the past behind us, Starling. You have a long life ahead of you and this could be the chance you need to really start living. You've been in hiding too long thanks to this group. Think about it—you could travel, see the world," Harper said, smiling.

"I could control the spirits," Starling said, her voice dreamy at the possibility of being free from the onslaught of voices.

Starling sat up from their huddle. "Give me the books and then draw up an official contract including the terms that all future drugs will be made through Harper's lab—you can negotiate your payment terms among yourselves. Deal?"

"We have to take a vote." President Kitchings stood up. "All of those in favor of making a peace treaty with the Sisterhood in exchange for the books and their giving us the medication and secrets we need, raise your hand."

Almost everyone in the room, except Virginia, raised their hand.

"It passes." President Kitchings motioned to Virginia. "Get her the books."

Virginia stood up and walked to the corner of the room where a picture of President Kitchings hung from the wall. Taking down the picture and dropping it with a clatter to the floor, she revealed a safe behind the portrait. She spun the dial and opened the metal vault. Starling sucked in a breath as the woman pulled out three large books and, shuffling her feet resignedly, brought them to the group. She thumped them on the black table in front of the president. "Here," she grunted, passing him a defiant look.

The books were smaller than Starling expected. For months, she had imagined them as if they were thousands of pages with heavy bindings and metal brackets. Instead they were thin, their edges curled with age. The covers were simple, each carrying nothing more than a trinity-like design. They looked antique, but aside from the cover they were *ordinary*. If Starling hadn't known the truth of what they were, it would have been hard to guess that these books held the secrets that would save her life.

"Thank you, Virginia." The president motioned for her to sit down and then turned back to Starling. "I believe these are the books you wanted." He pushed them across the table.

Starling picked the one on top. Its white velum cover was almost the same shade as her skin. The Red sat underneath, its cover the color of blood. Beneath it was the Black, its color so dark it almost disappeared into the table. She flipped open the White. Inside were hand-inked drawings and long pages filled with Latin.

Her knees weakened. The time had come … the books were here … in her hands. She sat down before her exhausted body failed.

"Are we allies?" the president asked.

Starling forced herself to stand back up and took his proffered hand. "Allies."

"What is the secret, Harper?"

"You must mate with a demigod while taking the pills," Harper said.

The door slammed open. Jim rushed into the room, Devon close behind him. Devon scanned the room, his eyes wild with rage.

"What's going on?" Jim screamed. "These are our enemies and you are having a meeting with them. That's bullshit! They deserve to die!"

Starling let go of President Kitchings's hand and moved down the table until she found the vulture's ruby-colored eye. She pressed down and frantically searched under the table with her left hand for another button, but she found nothing. She moved toward the gun, but Virginia stepped in her way. "Where's the elevator?" Starling yelled at the president.

"This table isn't an elevator. It's there—" He pointed to a large painting that adorned the wall.

"I'm not going in any damn elevator!" Jasper yelled. "There has to be another way!"

"Shut up! Everybody shut up!" Jim yelled.

Devon stared at her, the anger in his eyes turning to lust. Jasper pulled Starling down and pushed her to the floor. Her knees connected hard with the concrete.

"Don't touch her. Don't touch Starling!" Devon screamed. "She's mine!"

Starling watched in horror as Devon grabbed Jasper's gun and pointed it toward them.

The shot rang out, its deafening roar careening through the room.

Jasper crumpled to the ground beside her. A scream rippled from her lips as blood poured from his chest. "I … love … you." As the last word fell from his lips, his body stilled. His breathing stopped. Jasper was gone.

Starling pulled him against her chest as she rocked him back and forth in her arms. "You promised … you promised you wouldn't leave me … "

Chapter Twenty-One

Devon handed the gun to Jim and rushed to her side, dropping to his knees. "Sweetheart, are you okay?"

She stared at his eyes, noticing how the black had taken over. "You … you shot him." She looked away as the bitter taste of bile filled her mouth. Jasper lay in her arms, his head perched in the crook of her elbow. "Jasper, I'm so sorry," she whispered before leaning down to kiss his forehead. His skin was still warm, but even in its warmth it carried the weight of the dead.

"He threw you to the floor. No one can touch you like that. No one." Devon reached for her hand that rested on Jasper's motionless chest. She pulled away from his touch, hating him for making her move her hand from the man she loved.

"Get away," she said through her teeth.

"But … you love me. You and I, we can be together forever." The word *forever* hung in the air like the gun's smoke.

"I never want to be with you," she screamed.

Devon waved her off. "I was only protecting you. You will come to see that, sweetheart."

"You and your friends are to be arrested for murder and treason!" President Kitchings yelled above the melee of noise. "You shall be stripped of your feathers!"

Jim raised the gun, taking aim at the president. "Who's going to arrest me?" His finger moved under the trigger guard and Starling tensed, readying herself for the explosion.

"Jim, stop!" Virginia shouted. "You are not to hurt Steve."

Starling slipped her arm out from beneath Jasper's head and gently rested it on the ground. They had to pay. They had to pay for what they had done. "Devon?"

"Yes, sweetheart?" he asked.

"Get me that gun," she said, motioning toward Jim.

"Yes, sweetheart." Devon stood up and moved toward Jim.

She leaned down one more time and kissed Jasper's forehead. "I love you, Jasper. I'll always love you."

It was funny how much she had feared saying those words when he'd been alive, but now they flowed unchecked. Perhaps if she hadn't admitted it to herself, if she hadn't felt that love in the first place, he would have still been alive. But no. She had selfishly allowed herself to feel.

"Give me the gun, Jim," Devon said with outstretched hands.

"Shut up, Devon. You are as guilty as they are. You let her bewitch you. You promised you were better than this!"

"She's so beautiful. I love her." Devon signaled to Virginia to come closer. "Give me the gun, Jim, and I will let you run."

Virginia stood up and, brushing off her lap, she joined the middle-aged man. "I told you that you were better off staying with me, Starling. If you would have listened, maybe your little boyfriend would still be alive. There's really no one else to blame. You are responsible for his death."

"Shut up, bitch!" Starling jumped to her feet. "All you care about is yourself. In fact, you don't give a shit about Jim or Devon. You are only using them to get what you want."

"You mean like you are using Devon? Like you used Jasper?" Virginia retorted. "Devon, do you hear this? Do you understand that if you stay with her you will end up dead as well? There's no way out of here alive; she's a nymph. Nymphs leave only death behind. You must overthrow the spell the harlot has passed over you and choose our side, or you will end up like every other man nymphs have sunk their claws into."

Devon only gave Starling a bewitched, mindless smile.

"Go to hell! Go to hell!" A shrill non-human voice called from behind the room's closed doors.

The doors to the room flew open, one hitting Jim in the back and knocking him off balance. He staggered a few steps toward the table. Devon took his chance and grabbed the gun, stripping it clean of Jim's hands.

Standing in the doorway was Jamie, a gray parrot on her shoulder. Behind them were the Voodoo Queen Bethany, with her arm in a sling, and a dark-haired woman Starling didn't recognize.

"Go to hell!" the parrot repeated.

"How did you get in here?" Harper asked, choking back tears of relief.

"Bethany used her magic. What in the hell is going on here?" Jamie asked. She glanced around the room until her gaze settled on Devon and the gun in his hand. "Give me that."

"No. It's for Starling." He pulled the gun back against his chest protectively.

Jamie caught her eye, her gaze coming to a stop at the patch of fresh red blood on Starling's cloak and moving to Jasper, who lay limp in her arms. "Give me the gun." She stepped closer and grasped the gun in Devon's hands.

"No," he said, stepping back so his legs pressed against the side of the table.

"If you don't, Starling is going to get hurt." Jamie pulled the gun as Devon's grip weakened. "You don't want her to get hurt, do you?"

Devon released the gun, letting Jamie take it from him. "Good boy," she said, like he was nothing more than an obedient dog. She turned to Virginia, Jim, and the rest of the council. "Ariadne?" she asked, motioning for the woman behind her to step forward.

"Thank you, Jamie." Ariadne stopped beside Starling. She looked down at Jasper, pain radiating through her eyes. "He loved you, didn't he?"

Starling nodded. The axe of their curse had fallen.

"I'm more sorry than you can possibly know, Starling."

"Are you Ariadne Papadakis?"

The tanned, dark-haired woman nodded. "I'm here to help you." She glanced back down at Jasper. "I only wish I could have come sooner. Maybe we would have avoided this tragedy."

"Why did you bring Bethany here? She's my enemy."

Bethany ran her hand over the bandage on her shoulder where Starling had stabbed her. "You stabbed me. We be even."

"You tried to steal my friend. We're hardly even."

"You'd do anything to be with your lover. I'm no different, except my lover's gone."

Ariadne stepped between them. "Bethany was the only one who knew where we could find you and Harper. Without her and her magic, we never would have made it below. Mutual hatred makes great allies." Ariadne paused. "Don't worry, Starling, we will make this right and Bethany will help do that."

"Fine, but make no mistake, Bethany and I will never be friends." There was no making any of this right. Jasper was gone. Her love had killed him.

"Bethany says that you are responsible for erasing a soul. That type of action has consequences in the supernatural world. You are aware of this, are you not?" She turned as she addressed the council.

"It wasn't us," President Kitchings said, shaking his head. "It was Virginia and her group of followers. We never would have allowed such an action to be taken without a full vote."

Ariadne looked to Virginia. "Is that true? Did you take this action on your own without the support of your council?"

Virginia nodded. "You wouldn't understand ... "

"We will see that she and her lackeys are disciplined for their crimes," President Kitchings said. "What say you, council?"

The room filled with the members' agreement.

"She is your wife. How can I trust that you will give them the punishment they deserve?" Starling asked. "They killed him … " she sobbed.

Ariadne wrapped her arm around Starling. "It's okay. They will do what is right. Won't you?"

The president nodded. "On the subject of punishment for Virginia Kitchings, Jim Peterson, and Devon James, I move that we strip them each of their feathers and all rights given to our kind. They will no longer be allowed in or around any of our communities or their members. And from this day forth, they shall no longer be allowed to call or consider themselves Catharterians. What say you, council?"

He was answered with another round of unanimous "ayes."

Starling sucked in a long breath. Virginia, Jim, and Devon had lost everything. A shifter without their community would be at the mercy of the fates. They would no longer have the safety of their people and would be under the constant threat of other supernatural beings, beings that would love to enslave vultures and use them as they pleased. Yet, even with those staggering losses they still had their lives. The same couldn't be said for Jasper.

"Are you happy with that punishment?" President Kitchings asked.

Ariadne looked to her. "I know that it doesn't seem like enough. I know how badly it hurts right now, but killing them for what they have done won't bring Jasper back. It will only bring more death. They will no longer be supernatural. In time, their new level of humanity will bring its own justice."

Starling nodded. There would be no more death.

Chapter Twenty-Two

The taxi was cold even though the thick Savannah heat blanketed the world. Goose bumps rose over her body as she pulled Jasper's body tighter against her. The *Libros* collection stuck out of her purse and dug painfully into her side.

"Your friend is awfully quiet, ladies. He okay?" the taxi driver asked as he peered from Harper to Starling.

Jasper was perched in the back seat, his eyes closed, and his head resting on Starling's shoulder like he was merely asleep.

"He's fine," Harper replied from the front. She looked pointedly at the jacket Starling had put over Jasper's chest to hide the bullet wound. "Just drank too much."

The city twisted by, a world filled with deep early morning shadows, the kind that only further reminded Starling of how close they all were to the other side.

She should have taken the bullet for Jasper. She never should have gone for the elevator. She could have saved him, maybe not from her love, but at least from the bullet.

"Miss, you have something in your hair, ma'am." The cabby pointed to a spot near the front of his head. "Right there."

"Thanks." Reaching up, Starling pulled a black feather from her tresses. A slight sense of satisfaction whispered through her as she opened the car's window and pitched the feather into the wind.

"Make sure to stay behind that car," Starling said, motioning toward the black Escalade in front of them.

"You know where they are going, ma'am?"

"No idea." Bethany, Ariadne, and Jamie had been silent about their plans, only reassuring her that with the books everything would be okay. She found it hard to believe.

They made their way under a canopy of trees and past a long row of historical homes before the Escalade came to a stop beside Forsyth Park.

Harper glanced back at her and gave her a reassuring smile. "It will all be okay."

Her words sounded like the letter Epione had given Devon. "Absolutely." She smiled as a light breeze weaved through the moss that hung from the oaks, making them appear to give a welcoming wave.

The driver stepped out of the car and opened Starling's door. "Do you need help getting your friend somewhere? If you like, I could take him somewhere to let him sleep it off."

"No. We need to take him to the fountain," Harper said as she came around the car.

Ariadne, Bethany, and Jamie made their way out of the black Escalade and walked back to her taxi. "We'll help her," Ariadne said with a soft smile.

"Are you sure you ladies can handle him, ma'am?" he asked.

"One man? That's nothing." Harper laughed as she handed the man the money for their fare. "Please load all of the luggage into their car. We'll be fine from here."

"Got it, ma'am," the driver said, turning from their small group of women.

Starling stepped out of the car.

"I got his arms. You got his legs?" Starling asked Ariadne as she slipped her hands under Jasper's arms.

In her wildest nightmares, Starling never would have believed that she would someday ask the leader of the Sisterhood to help carry her dead lover.

Bethany and Jamie helped slide Jasper out of the car and, with each of them holding on, they carried him to the fountain and laid him on the ground.

"Why did we need to bring him here?" Starling wiped the sweat from her brow.

The fountain's underwater lights were still on, giving off a haunting glow.

Jamie brushed her hands clean. "Savannah's a special place, with special magic. Didn't you feel it when you got here?"

Starling thought back to the moment she had stepped out of the airport, the feel of the moist swamp air and the winds that hinted of potential for change. She nodded.

"This place, this wonderful park has absorbed some of the happiness that goes on 'round here. All that good energy builds up, makin' this the place you want to be when you want good things to come back to you."

"What's going to happen?" Starling pressed.

"Only your goddess can answer that." Jamie said with a mischievous smile. "You must trust in her; she has shown me what is to come."

"They be here ... " Bethany looked around like she could see things others could not.

"Who?" Starling asked.

I promised I would be waiting... Asclepius's spectral voice filled her mind.

"She be comin' soon," Bethany whispered.

"Who?"

Asclepius's ghostly figure stepped out from behind a large oak near the fountain. "My wife," he said as he stroked his long beard..

"Who's your wife?"

"Your goddess. My Epione. Have I never told you?" He smiled gently. "Did you get the books?"

"Yes, and I'm going to use them to stop you from ever bothering me again." She reached down and drew the Black from her purse and laid it on the ground next to Jasper's body.

"I think you will come to regret having said that. Do you know why Zeus sent me to the Underworld?"

Starling shook her head. "What does that have to do with you being here?"

"Zeus was angry when Artemis came to me and offered me gold to resurrect Hippolytus." Asclepius glanced up at the sculpture of the woman at the top of the fountain.

"You bring the dead back to life? Can you bring Jasper back to life?" She had learned her lesson for hoping, but this time she couldn't help herself. She had to hope for Jasper's return. She needed him back.

"I could, but only when I was alive."

Her heart sank at his rejection. "If you can't help me bring Jasper back, why are you here?"

"I wish to help. You have great potential."

The wind shifted directions and it blew a faint mist off the water, the moisture wetting her face, drawing her attention to the fountain. The white, iron woman at the top shifted. Her hand, holding the iron dress above her knee, loosened and the changing fabric dropped to her ankle. Her face transformed. The lines of the woman's face softened and her lips turned up into an easy smile. "Starling, my dear, you must trust my husband. He only wishes to help. Just as I do." Epione floated down, rod in hand, and stopped beside Starling on the sidewalk. "We will make everything right just as Ariadne has promised."

Epione waved for the other women to step nearer. "Lay your hands on Jasper's body. We need your power." She gestured to Starling. "You need to put your hand over his heart."

Starling put her hands on Jasper's chest. "I can't do this ... I don't have enough power."

"You must trust in your gift, Starling. Your ability is strong. You just have to believe." Asclepius flipped the book open and pointed down at the page. "Read the words."

Starling turned to the page and ran her finger over the black-inked words. Even though she didn't know their meaning, they looked beautiful in the way they scrolled across the page.

Spiritus, convenientibus terra viventium. Restitue animam et corpus. Benedictus in sæcula. Gratia. Misericordia. Amor ... .

"In order for it to work, you must believe. You must have full intention." Asclepius kneeled beside her and placed his hands next to hers on Jasper's chest. The woman all followed his lead until each were touching Jasper.

Could she do what the ghost wanted of her? Three months ago, sitting in her family's apartment in Vegas, she would have never believed she had the power to control anything—not spirits, not spells, and barely even her own emotions. Yet, this morning, with her fingers touching the still chest of the man she loved, she knew she had found power in her moments of weakness. She had overthrown her enemies, she had found justice when there seemed there would be none. She had changed.

She closed her eyes and concentrated on her words. "Spiritus, convenientibus terra viventium. Restitue animam et corpus. Benedictus in sæcula. Gratia. Misericordia. Amor."

Power ran through her hands and she repeated the words again. The power amplified, drawing from her heart and draining through her fingers. There was a collective gasp from the other women as they, too, must have felt the power flow.

Jasper inhaled deeply. A pink hue returned to his cheeks and his eyes fluttered open. "Starling?" he whispered. "Starling, are you okay?"

The others sat back, taking their hands from Jasper. Asclepius moved beside Epione and laid his wraithlike hand upon hers.

A tear of relief slipped down her cheek. "Jasper ... You're back. You're ... you're alive," she stammered. She lowered her forehead, touching it against his steadily warming cheek. "I love you." She kissed his cheek. "I love you."

"I love you, too." Jasper reached up and wrapped his arms around her.

"I'm so sorry. I'm so sorry I let this happen to you."

"Don't be sorry. I sacrificed myself to protect you. I kept you safe. I would give my life again." He drew in a long breath, filling his lungs. "Though, next time, I'll get in the damn elevator."

"Next time, I'll keep Jamie's stone," she said, looking toward the psychic.

Jamie nodded, smiling. "A new one is on the house."

"As luck would have it," Epione said, drawing Starling's attention, "you'll never have to worry about giving up your life again. Thanks to Starling, you have joined the ranks of the near immortal. Because she cast the spell, you will have her same weakness—if someone pulls your hair, you will die, but if you protect your weakness, you will be able to live forever ... forever at Starling's side."

"But what about the curse of our kind?" Ariadne asked.

"This can't happen again. Zeus can't do this to another of our kind. He has to be stopped," Starling said.

Epione gave them a knowing look. "That is a war we will need to fight. All of us. Together. First, we need to gain strength. We need to unify. Do you think you can do that, Ariadne?"

"Yes. I can't think of many who would object to the fight."

"In the meantime, Starling, I must ask a favor of you."

"Anything for my goddess," Starling said, her tears of relief and joy steadily slipping down her cheeks as she stared at Jasper's full lips.

"Would you please help me?" Asclepius asked. "I wish to join my wife, and should you and your kind choose, your fight as well."

Starling nodded. "Ladies, let's hold hands. We need to repeat the spell for Asclepius. He wishes to no longer be merely a ghost."

She gave Jasper a soft kiss to the cheek and stood up. "Stand in the middle of the circle, Asclepius."

The ghost drifted to the center of the women as they all joined hands.

"Spiritus convenientibus terra viventium. Restitue animam et corpus. Benedictus in sæcula. Gratia. Misericordia. Amor," the women said in unison.

The wind around them sped up and twisted. In the center of the circle, Asclepius's body started to form from his ghostly features. His gray-speckled beard filled out and his face took on the hue of sun-warmed honey. Gone was the mistiness of his wraith form.

Asclepius ran to Epione and took her in his arms. "My love," he whispered, pressing his lips to hers. He looked over to the women. "I knew you were the one, Starling."

"The one?" Starling let go of Jamie's hand and returned to Jasper's side.

"Yes," Asclepius replied, drawing Epione deeper into his arms. "You are the one who is going to save us all."

She didn't know if she believed him, but it didn't matter. She had tapped into her powers. She had the man she loved—a man who was now nearly immortal.

"One more thing," Epione said, stepping out of Asclepius's arms with a quick kiss. "You have proven yourself a woman of great strength, courage, and character. As such, I'm honored to give you the gift of the mark."

"The mark?" Jasper asked.

"Every nymph has a tattoo of their totem animal," Starling explained. "For me, it's the swan."

"Are you ready?" Epione asked.

Starling lowered the edge of her dress, exposing the back of her neck. Epione touched the spot gently. There was a flash of warmth as the ink moved through her skin, forming her black swan.

"Be proud. You are Nymph. You are a demigod. You are my sister," Epione said with a slight bow.

"Thank you."

"You're welcome. You deserve the world for returning my love to me." Epione tipped her head in acknowledgment and returned to Asclepius.

Jasper wrapped his arms around Starling from behind and kissed the edges of her ears. "I don't know that I'm the world, but I will give you everything I can."

"I don't want everything," Starling said, turning around in his arms to face him. "I only want you, my shadow."

About the Author

Danica Winters is a bestselling author of more than ten books. She has won multiple awards and is known for writing books that grip readers with their ability to drive emotion through suspense and occasionally a touch of magic. Most recently, Danica was the winner of the 2013 Paranormal Romance Guild's Book of the Year Award and is currently a finalist in the Chanticleer Book Reviews Paranormal Awards of 2013 for her paranormal romantic suspense novel, *Montana Mustangs*.

When she's not working, she can be found in the wilds of Montana testing her patience while she tries to understand the allure of various crafts (quilting, pottery, and painting are not her thing). She always believes the cup is neither half full nor half empty, but it better be filled with wine.

More from This Author
(From *Winter Swans* by Danica Winters)

The chapel of the funeral home was filled with familiar faces, each one drawn into a somber expression as they wandered past Harper Cygnini's sister's casket. A blonde nymph laid a single crystal swan inside the box, carefully placing the bird by the hundreds of others. The bird sat with its wings touching those of the one next to it, looking as if they would come alive and fly Jenna to the realm of the gods.

Harper stood at the head of the casket and shook hands as people passed by, never looking her in the eyes. There were no words to express the sadness that filled the room. This didn't happen. Nymphs rarely died.

She dabbed at her stinging eyes. She had cried so much in the last week it came as a shock to her there were any tears left to be shed. Her heart wasn't merely broken—no, the pain ran much deeper—it was almost as if she had died as well. Maybe she should have—the gods knew she deserved to be struck down. If she had just been more involved with her sister, if she had paid more attention, perhaps this would have never happened. She could have stopped her sister from being kidnapped. She would have noticed that Jenna had been missing. Instead Harper had merely gotten the call that Jenna's body had been found frozen in a snow bank on some mountain.

The only comfort she could find was that the men responsible had been incarcerated and awaited trial in Montana. They would pay for their atrocious crimes.

The only man in the room, Beau Morris, sat next to his fiancée, Ariadne Papadakis, the leader of the Sisterhood of Epione. Ariadne, noticing Harper's gaze, dipped her head in a humble tribute to

Jenna. Harper recognized a few of the other women within the room as mustang, snake, and swan-shifters. It was easy to tell them from the non-supernatural attendees as, even in mourning, most nymphs were perfectly beautiful—unscathed by time and the ravages of living.

The same couldn't be said of Harper, but she didn't care. She glanced down at her black dress. She couldn't remember putting it on or doing her hair, but what did it matter? Even as a demigod life was short and filled with pain. What difference did her appearance really make—it was like so many other unimportant things that both humans and nymphs seemed to deem worthwhile. She couldn't strike the impious thought that life was only some god's sick joke—they merely sat up in the heavens playing around with everyone's lives, striking down those who displeased them and testing to see how much pain those that remained could withstand.

A hand touched her shoulder, making her jerk to attention.

"Harper?" a redheaded woman asked. She was beautiful and clearly a nymph, but she didn't have the same youthful, healthy glow of the others that filled the room. Instead her face was thin and her eyes tired.

"Yes. Thank you for coming to show your respect," she answered robotically as she readied herself for more well-deserved but undesired condolences.

"I'm Carey Jackson, a friend … I mean I *was* a friend of your sister."

The words pierced Harper's armor and drove straight to her heart. The tears stung her tired eyes. She could only nod, or any control she had would be lost.

Carey dropped her hand from Harper's shoulder. "I'm sorry to have to do this to you, but your sister was my landlord and, well, she promised she would help me. And now I don't have anyone to turn to, except you."

Harper looked around, checking to see if what she was hearing was really happening here, at her sister's funeral. Some of the pain she had been feeling dissipated and was replaced by red-hot anger. "You can't be serious. You didn't come here to ask for a favor. You didn't come to this place … and this time … and want to *use* my sister's death to your advantage. No one can be that callous."

The redhead stepped back from the onslaught of verbal strikes. "I'm … I'm sorry. I didn't mean to upset you. I just need help. You don't understand."

Harper's gaze dropped to Jenna. Her makeup was perfectly applied and her pale face unmoving, as if she had merely fallen asleep. Her brunette hair haloed around her and, even though she lay there in the white metal box, it was still hard to believe she was really gone.

Carey reached into her purse and pulled out a picture. "I'm looking for this man. I need to find him, it's important. Please."

Harper didn't know what to say. She knew her anger toward the woman was based mostly in her own grief. The redhead needed help, even if she had made a mistake in approaching her here on this day.

Carey offered her the picture. Harper looked down at the image—the man was muscular and tan, almost the color of fresh honey. His copper-tinted brown hair framed his face and accentuated his stubble-covered jaw. He was laughing at some secret joke that had been lost in time and only his smile was preserved. She flipped over the picture and scrawled across the back was the name Chance Landon.

"Look," she started. "I don't think I can help … " She glanced up, but the redhead was gone. The next mourner in line, a petite woman with a sharp beak-like nose, stepped forward.

"Where … " Harper looked past the mousy haired woman in front of her in search of the mysterious redhead.

"Excuse me?" the mousy woman said with an out-of-place smile.

"Yes, sorry," Harper said, forcing herself to look at the gray business suit clad woman in front of her. The top button of the woman's white dress shirt was fastened and there wasn't a wrinkle to be seen anywhere on her perfectly put together outfit. "Thank you for coming." The practiced words tumbled from her lips.

"You are welcome. I just wanted to introduce myself. I'm Dr. Redbird. I was the chief medical examiner on your sister's case."

Harper tried to keep the shock from striking her down. So many emotions invaded her all at once. Anger. Pain. Resentment. Thankfulness. "What are you doing here?"

The woman's smile flickered and she glanced over her shoulder, like she was looking for some kind of attack. "I just wanted to say how sorry I am for your sister's death. I thought I would pay my last respects to her family … and your kind."

Something about the woman seemed *off*, but then again everything that was happening in Harper's life didn't seem to fit. She'd never prepared herself to be standing in a room full of acquaintances, mourners, and a favor-asking redhead—especially when they were all there to pay respects to her sister, a woman she had thought would never die.

Also check out these Danica Winters titles:

Montana Mustangs

The Nymph's Labyrinth

In the mood for more Crimson Romance?
Check out *Starlaw* by Candace Sams at *CrimsonRomance.com*.